Chinz

The Perfect Coffee

A pot of life

AF237400

„Dreams with the scent of coffee are always good dreams."

Author

Chinz, born in Cologne 1968, dwells in Varel.

He works as a nurse, lives as a musician and author and describes himself as a melancholy in a good mood.

Released so far:

- „Alzagra", Novel
- „Die Brücke", Crime story
- „Fast zu spät", Novel
- „Ruhe sanft", Crime story
- „Die Besucher", Play
- „Jupp", Novella
- „Der perfekte Kaffee", Novel
- „Das Buch der Unruhe des Hilfsmelancholikers Leon Sersoa", Novel

Chinz

The Perfect Coffee

A pot of life

Translated by Marcus Brody

Tiff & Toff Taschenbuch 011

Die Deutsche Nationalbibliothek verzeichnet diese Publikation in der Deutschen Nationalbibliografie; detaillierte bibliografische Daten sind im Internet über http://dnb.dnb.de abrufbar.

© 2020 by Chinz und Tiff & Toff – Verlag
Hullenwiesenstraße 8
26316 Varel
www.TiffundToff-Verlag.de

Herstellung und Verlag:
BoD – Books on Demand, Norderstedt
ISBN: 978-3-7526-4734-1

for my muse

Prologue

The young man with the dark hair sat on the table diagonally across from me. In the beginning, I only looked at him because I was jealous. His table stood in the sun, while I was freezing in the shadow on this, for the beginning of July, unusually cold day.

It took me a while to realise why I could not take my eyes off him and why, when he had finished his coffee, felt warm as well.

He had a big pot of coffee and a small jug with milk on his table. Prior to every sip he looked into his cup, added some milk or coffee from the pot, stirred briefly, looked again and adjusted it once more if need be – like a painter, unhappy with the colour or intensity of the painting, adding another layer.

Before actually drinking, he closed his eyes, smelled the coffee and then took, slowly and gently, almost tenderly, a sip. The cup always remained at his lips for a long time and his face would tell a story. Intense emotions of joy, hope, love and happiness.

He seemed to be far away in his thoughts; did not notice anything that was happening around him – not the noisy rattling when the waitress dropped her tray behind him, nor the bawling toddler in the passing pram.

While at first, I had thought he was enjoying an extraordinarily well crafted coffee, by the end of it I understood: He had just emptied a cup containing his entire life. As if the movie we supposedly see before our mind's eye, in the moment of our death, had played for him, while drinking this pot of coffee ...

„To drink up one's life" – is a less than perfect way to put it, but that is what it felt like, literally. Perhaps because every time I looked at him, I had the feeling that he had grown older. It was either the sun blinding me in the beginning or, while drinking, he had matured by several decades. Actually, sitting there was a man with silver hair and quite a few wrinkles to his face.

What did happen to him, after he had emptied the last sip?

I do not know. I had tried in the meantime to experience something similar while drinking my coke. And while refreshing and sparkling, nothing much happened in my imagination when I closed my eyes – I saw myself sitting in the shadow, shivering and drinking coke.

I looked to the man once more and while he was mixing the colour, this time with so much milk that the coffee had to come out grey or white, I realised my mistake. Slowly I lifted my glass, took a lengthy look at the colour of my lemonade (hoping nobody was watching me doing so), closed my eyes and, slowly and gently, took a sip of the sticky sugar water ...

I was back in art class, on the left behind Susan, whose dark auburn hair actually had a resemblance to the colour of coke, I never had noticed before. Even in my memory the class was sticky as it always had been and just like the drink in my mouth now. But the way I saw Susan this time, serene, in profile, all of a sudden I had a very clear understanding of what a true piece of art really is.

I swallowed the coke, Susan turned around, a cool, refreshing tingling in my throat, a hot, exhilarating shiver on my back.

When I opened my eyes again, he was gone.

The waitress was clearing his pot onto a tray. I quickly looked around, but even in the street he was nowhere to be seen.

For some reason, I harbour the honest belief that, after taking the last sip of his coffee, he had just, no not just, but with a happy and satisfied smile, after a long and fulfilling life, vanished into thin air ...

Sip One

Somewhere in the world the sun was shining.

People were lying on the beach, walking through fields of flowers in full bloom or had a refreshing drink on the patio.

Somewhere in the world the sun was shining right now.

Somewhere ..., far ..., very far away.

Ted turned on the windshield wipers, closed his eyes, annoyed from the squeaking sound, took a deep breath, opened his eyes again, drove the five metres up to the Vauxhall Astra in front of him, stopped and turned off the wipers.

Nothing but rain since Oberhausen, two hundred kilometres left to Hamburg and already four construction sites.

Half a minute later, the Astra drove another twenty metres, before stopping again.

Can I manage such a long journey, or should I rest after the first ten metres?

Ted turned the wiper on again and put the pedal to the metal.

With any other car that would have been overkill, but his Volkswagen bus had considerable trouble to get going up a hill; even on full throttle it bucked heavily.

The wiper blades were squeaking so loudly that there was no enjoyment to be had from listening to music. Ted turned off the tape deck and drove the twenty metres.

This time the VW bus bucked even when he hit the brakes.

Ted was considerably behind schedule. The rest of the band was most likely scrambling into the rehearsal room at this moment and wondering why the guitars and amplifiers had not arrived yet. Without him they would not be able to start and they really needed to practice before the concert tomorrow!

The performance in Munich had been a disaster. They had been playing together for three years now, always the same, original songs, that were not that hard to begin with but still ... Yesterday had been their first time in front of a large audience – almost a thousand people in the venue – and Bernd and Peter had cracked. When drums and bass constantly drop out of the rhythm, there is nothing much that guitar and piano can do.

The Losers would have been a more than fitting band name yesterday. It was one of the names up for discussion when they first got together; in the end though, they had settled for *The Flying Dishes*.

Tomorrow, in Hamburg, they expected over two thousand spectators, among them some professional critics, maybe even a record label executive ... their big break.

Finally, smooth sailing. But now the VW bus was bucking even while travelling an even road.

Ted once again turned on the cassette tape with the demo of a new song, that he was going to show to the others in a moment. The melody had been stuck in his head for ages, the lyrics not so much.

He still needed a fitting comparison for the last verse.

Her hair as auburn as Madagascar ebony wood ...

That of course was only a temporary version. He actually had never met anyone, who was familiar with the typical dark brown, almost black hue of Madagascar ebony wood. It did not rhyme and in no way fit the rhythm. But it was after all Julia's hair colour, his first girlfriend, to whom the song was dedicated.

Hazard lights in front of him, again ... the next traffic jam. Ted shook his head in frustration. For some reason he had thought that hardly anybody lived up north and those few who did either drove their tractors far from the motorway or were already at home at this hour.

Police and ambulance passed him by on the emergency lane but other than that there was no movement.

A little while later another ambulance and a fire truck. Apparently a severe accident, possibly complete closure. Without much success Ted tried to find a radio station reporting traffic news, or to be more precise, to find any radio station.

Several cars passed him by on the emergency lane. There had to be an exit ahead.

Ted took his road map from the glove compartment. This would be a major detour, through several, to him completely unknown villages, but much more preferable than standing around here for what could easily be another few hours.

The country road kept going for, what felt like twenty kilometres, when finally the first actual turn came up and a short way after that ... the street was closed for construction work!

Shit! Brown like shit!

Two alternative routes were signposted, one to the right, one to the left, both to places he did not know ... His map was old, the light in the bus could hardly be called one and the rain had become heavier. Street names were unreadable.

Some country road, somewhere in Ostfriesland, torrential rain, thunder and lightning.

Ted closed his eyes for a moment, asked his instincts who just shrugged in uncertainty.

Ted took the left turn into a bumpy, unlit way. A sign warned him of roadway damage.

The VW bus and the potholes duked it out for several kilometres, who could produce the stronger bucking, until the bus gave up, not just the competition – it was no longer bucking ..., in fact, it was not doing much of anything anymore. Ted floored the pedal, but the engine died, and the bus rolled for another few metres and then just sat there.

Nothing.

Where was he? Somewhere in no-man's-land.

No town. Anywhere.

A blinding flash of light immediately followed by a deafening bang. The lightning bolt had split a tree only about fifty metres from where he was sitting. Under other circumstances an impressive display. But Ted was only thinking of the headline of this morning's newspaper:

Not all vehicles safe in a thunderstorm!

He actually had not read the article itself.

He was scared.

Five minutes later the storm had passed, and the rain started to let up. Ted got out and opened the bonnet. He took one look in the engine bay and shrugged. What had he expected? He had no idea whatsoever of cars, had never even changed a tyre or oil in his life. There seemed to be an engine, possibly, something in the dark that looked like it.

He slammed the bonnet shut. Even if he had had an idea ... It was pitch black, he did not have a torch and the rain was picking up again. He sat back in the bus; the windows fogged up in a matter of seconds.

Ted took his guitar and played the new song.

Brown like shit even fit the rhythm. Although it did not quite fit the initial intentions he had had for the song.

Ted put the guitar aside and looked at his watch. Right about now rehearsals should have started. He had an inkling about what the others were saying about him at this moment.

The atmosphere had been tense for weeks.

The words „break-up" had not yet been uttered by any of them but Ted was sure that he was not alone in having thought about it. It was likely that the others would prefer to go on without him. He might have been the founder of the band and had written most of the songs on the first album but the happier, more successful songs from the second were Bernd's.

If Ted was honest with himself, he had lost all will to play with the others, but he saw no alternative.

A solo career? His songs were written for a band, maybe for a nice night around a campfire.

Ted was staring out the window, without noticing that he really was not staring out the window but was merely looking at the fogged up glass ... - it did not make much of a difference, everything outside was grey and wet as well.

Forming a new band would take time; what would he live off and where?

Back to his parents? They would be grateful!

Yes ..., sure ..., they probably would be indeed, but what about himself?

His parents were his past, his mostly unpleasant past. Music was his life but to be able to live off that now seemed more unlikely than ever before. Which was only made worse by the memory of his father telling him so.

Finally some light. The sky was partially breaking open. Every now and then the moon could be seen.

Ted had been standing here for over half an hour but not a single car had passed him by during that time.

He got out. As far as he remembered, there had been no lit houses for the past few kilometres, so he went the other way.

Gone was the rain and in its stead a strong, icy wind had picked up; every now and then lightning in the distance, low rumbling sky.

Ted could not help but think of the split-up with Julia. Then too had he walked home on a cold and dark night, for half an hour through storm and rain.

Only this time not only wouldn't he be home after half an hour; so far he had not even encountered any signs of life in this part of the world.

What if there were not any houses for hours to come?

His clothes were soaked, and he was shaking from the cold. Go back?

The bus was not offering any warmth either.

Ted went on, without feeling that he made any progress.

The shaking became stronger, his teeth would have chattered if it were not for the fact that he clenched his mouth shut and his thoughts grew increasingly melodramatic:

Is this the end?

With every flash of lightning another memory came to him.

If this is my life flashing before my eyes, it is rather sobering.

But dying? Just when I thought the great, free life was about to be ... There!!!

Up ahead was a village!

In the brief illumination of another lightning, Ted had spotted the outlines of a church tower. He walked faster.

Twenty minutes later he finally reached an inhabited area. A few dark houses, the church tower could be made out as a shadow and a lit pub.

Ted was only steps away from the *Kyffhaus Hut*, when there too the lights went off.

No!

Ted ran the last hundred metres to the building. A weak light was still burning within the bar. He knocked on the window until the door was opened a gap.

„Sorry, we're closed!"

„I'm sorry to bother you! My car broke down and I need to use a phone! Would that be possible? Please! I'll be gone the moment I'm done!"

Ted could not make out anything in the dark gap in front of him.

For a moment nothing happened.

„Okay. One moment."

The chain was pulled from the door and it swung open. A small dark-haired woman, around his age stood in front of Ted and gave him a smile.

„Come on in."

„Thanks. Thank you very much!"

Ted wiped his muddy shows extensively on the doormat and walked into the bar. All chairs had been turned up onto the tables and the barstools stood on the counter. The young woman sized him up.

„You've been out in the rain for a while now, haven't you? Quite a bit of shit weather we're having today!"

„You can say that again!" Ted had a hard time keeping his teeth from chattering. „Where is the phone?"

„Behind the bar, on the left. Just dial zero and you're good to go. Do you have any change?"

„Yes. Thanks!"

Kira had taken a look around the inside of the bus and was just about to climb back out again.

„We have two guestrooms at the *Kyffhaus Hut* and they're both free."

She gave the man her phone number, for the garage to call, when the bus was ready; then walked back to her car with Ted and drove back to the pub.

She took the key from a key box next to the door.

„The code is easy to remember: My mother loves *Eau de Cologne* – so it's *4711*."

She just made a little light in the bar, with several candles at a table.

„Do you want a beer or whisky to wash down the news?"

„Thanks. But I think I'd prefer another coffee."

„Gladly! I'll have another one as well."

They sat down with their coffee at the candlelit table.

Ted let out a satisfied sigh after his first sip: „Tastes exceptionally good."

„This one really is something special. Coming from a little coffee farm near the Kilimanjaro. A woman from this area migrated there ten years ago, started a little coffee farm and now sells her coffee all over the world. We are the only place in the area, that serves coffee from the *Machare-Farm*. For a while, I was entertaining the thought of running away from home, somehow making my way to Tanzania and to find work on that farm, but I didn't dare."

„Well, I did run away from home to live my dream, but that never really ... Oh well ... Sorry, I wasn't trying to talk you out of it!"

„No worries. It was more of an escapist dream rather than my life's calling and now my liberation from this backwater town is almost in sight. So your dream was to become a musician?"

"Yes."

"And you play in a band?"

"Yes. How did you ...?"

"Your bus is full of guitars and parts of your phone call were impossible to miss. You guys have a problem?"

"Yes. We were supposed to rehearse tonight for the show tomorrow. We're playing a concert in Hamburg."

"Cool! Though ..., tomorrow? What a shame! I can't make it tomorrow; you guys play any more?"

"No. It was supposed to be the highlight and grand finale of the tour; but if we ever play again like we did in Munich, it is more likely going to be the finale of our careers."

Ted briefly told her some of what happened at the concert, Kira only said: "Oh boy!", then both went silent and drank hot coffee.

Even though Ted could now see the whole of the catastrophe staring him in the face, he felt better.

"What's the name of your band?"

"The Flying Dishes."

"No way! Then you're Ted Schäffler?"

"Yes."

"Blimey! I must have listened to *Homecoming Queen* at least a thousand times by now."

"You have?"

"Yes. I love that song! Can you play it on the piano?"

"No, only on guitar. Do you have one?"

"Crying shame! If only we had brought one of yours! We only have a piano here. But ... Can you tell me the chords?"

20

Kira sat down at the piano at the end of the room, Ted stood next to her and told her how he played it on guitar. Kira 'translated' the chords effortlessly for the piano and it was not long and both of them were singing *Homecoming Queen* and a few other songs of the first album.

Kira was beaming. „Come on, have a go! The song really isn't all that hard. Basically, all you need is four chords and a few bridges. I'll teach you in no time."

Ted had a seat on the piano stool. Twelve times had he been seated on such a piece of furniture, his piano teacher standing diagonally behind him. Even without looking, he had felt her disappointed face behind him.

„Oh bugger! You used to have piano lessons?"

„Yes."

„Okay. You *can* position your hands like that ..., if you're planning on working through the notes as planned and like a good student, but ..., if you want to live the music, I recommend a more relaxed position of the hands and the whole body. You haven't sat up this straight all evening! Do you really want to sit like that?"

„Well ... Er ... No."

„Forget everything you ever learned. Music doesn't want to be worked off according to plan, it wants to be discovered. Be you. Play, how it is comfortable for you, intuitively."

Ted looked at the piano and his hands quite puzzled, tried to ease up inside, to think of nothing, but he failed. At the very least he managed, after taking two deep breaths, to banish his old piano teacher from his thoughts and to notice the new one next to him ... and the scent of coffee in the air. Ted looked at Kira, smiling at him amicably, took another sip from his cup and began to play.

It sounded horrible.

The piano teacher showed not a hint of disappointment on her face:

„Very good! That was a start! You broke free from your petrification. Now you only need to find your way. I am going to try something."

Kira seated herself behind him on the chair and led his hands.

At first Ted had troubles to give himself to the music. He felt Kira's warm hands on his own; her breasts caressing his back; hear breath on his neck and, as if that were not confusing enough already, a never known sensation of safety and home.

No, he was not interested in music in the least right now; at least not in how it might sound for others, whether he was playing correctly or somebody was making a disappointed face.

He had given up all efforts, was not paying attention to how his fingers moved, just let Kira lead and the music happen.

After playing together for several minutes, Kira let go of his hands and Ted noticed to his astonishment that his fingers simply kept playing on, without him taking control or having to think about it.

Before, music had always been something on the outside of himself, something he tried to invent and give form. Now it was inside himself, he did not invent, he discovered. A world inside himself, he could have never guessed existed.

And ... There was a completely new sound. The old songs, he had played hundreds of times, sounded completely different, as if they had just now found their meaning.

Kira was still seated quietly behind him, her arms wrapped around his body and her head resting against his back.

After playing all his old songs, he tried the new one. And this one too sounded worlds better on the piano, than it did on the guitar. For the first time Kira raised her head again:

„That is beautiful! That is ... I don't know that one. What's the name? Is it new?"

„Yes. It's new and not quite finished. *Julia* is what it's going to be called. It was meant for guitar, but I haven't made any progress on it for months. And now ..."

She nodded.

„The right thing with the wrong instrument. A rarely noticed yet profound problem in the world. You write all songs?"

„Only a few. *Homecoming Queen* ... Most songs on the first album."

„But it was great. Your second album though, *Blockbuster*, is not for me really."

They played a few more songs for each other, until they, at just about three a.m., in spite of another cup of coffee, were both too tired to continue.

Kira showed Ted to the guest room and noticed that the beds were not yet made. With tired eyes she looked at him: „No way I'm doing that now. You haven't fallen over me so far; I doubt you'll do it in my room. The bed is rather big anyway ... You promise to be good?"

„Not an easy promise to make, but tiredness is on your side."

Kira fell asleep quickly.

Ted was tired as well but at the same time had a strong desire to return to the piano and keep discovering the new world that had just opened up in front of him. But not only would that wake up Kira ..., getting up was impossible, because of what he was looking at sleeping next to him.

Kira's beautiful, completely serene face was lying so close to his. Her lips were slightly apart, as if they were waiting for his kiss. Was there maybe another world, waiting for him to explore it?

Ted felt the strong urge to kiss her and thought it over again and again, what had Kira meant when she had told him to be good ...; and pondering he fell asleep.

Sometime later that night, Ted woke up and noticed that Kira was now in his arms, her head on his chest. He gently squeezed her, but Kira was fast asleep.

Ted felt her calm, peaceful breath and again this supreme feeling of home. He kissed her softly, buried his face in her wild, auburn hair, still rich with the scent of coffee and fell asleep again.

When Ted woke up the next morning from the ringing of the alarm, he felt Kira's hand in his own. Other than that, they both were lying each on their respective side of the bed. Ted was not fully sure, whether her head on his chest tonight had been a dream or reality.

Slowly Kira opened her eyes. Ted gently squeezed her hand. She looked surprised, squeezed back and smiled at him, while their hands parted:

„Good morning, Ted!"

He answered, his voice slightly croaking: „Good morning, Kira."

„Coffee?"

„Absolutely!"

„Stay in bed a little while longer. I'll freshen up and make us some coffee."

Only a short while later, Kira returned, freshly showered, her hair fixed and with two steaming cups of coffee.

It were the same cups from last night: On Kira's cup was Snoopy, on the roof of his house and on Ted's was Linus with his blankey.

For the duration of the coffee, they sat, mostly silent, both still a bit fuzzy but happily smiling, next to each other on the edge of the bed.

„Thanks for letting me stay the night."

„Oh, my pleasure really! I slept like a rock. You were playing the piano for me in my dreams tonight. It was nice."

„I slept well too; but was dreaming more of coffee rather than the piano. Does your hair smell of coffee by any chance?"

„They do indeed", Kira nodded and bowed her head to Ted, so he could take a whiff.

„I spiced up my shampoo a little. I always have coffee with me that way. I like the scent of coffee even better than its taste. Especially when opening a new pack ... Hang on. I think, I have to refill anyway."

Kira went downstairs and returned a moment later with an empty pack that had held coffee beans only a moment ago.

„Sit down in that chair over there and close your eyes."

Ted took a seat in the comfortable chair next to the bed and closed his eyes.

„What am I supposed to do now?"

„Hold the pack under your nose, breath in and out deeply and see what happens."

Ted held the empty pack of coffee under his nose and took in deeply the fresh, intense scent of the coffee beans.

The pictures in his head became clearer and at the same time, warmer and softer. He saw himself again on the way back from Julia; but the rain was no longer cold and hitting him in the face. It was a gentle summer rain, caressing the skin, refreshing it and he went home, thinking of all the nice weeks they had lived, loved and enjoyed together.

Ted opened his eyes. Kira looked at him expectantly.

„Well ...?"

„That was ... Truly remarkable!"

Ted had a refreshed feeling on his skin, in all the places the rain had touched him in his memory just a moment ago.

„I have never had such a clear image when dreaming."

Kira beamed at him. „Excellent! Then let's try the main event."

Kira handed Ted his cup.

„Take a sip first and then a whiff?"

„No. First smell it for a long time, then take a sip, keep it in your mouth and move it around."

„...and wait for what happens."

„Precisely."

„I can't wait. Do you only have pleasant dreams, while doing that?"

„Dreams with the scent of coffee are always good dreams."

In the beginning, Ted felt a strong desire to move his dreams in the direction of the events of last night, but instead he saw himself standing on a stage in Hamburg. The Flying Dishes started playing, their songs sounded better than ever before, Ted's guitar solo went better than ever ..., but when looking through the audience, he noticed in horror that only a single person had come ... No, not in horror at all. It was Kira! He waved at her, she waved back and then he put his hand back on the piano ... Piano? Hadn't he been playing the guitar only a moment ago? Where were his bandmates? No, only the both of them remained and Madagascar ebony-wood rhymed beautifully all of a sudden ... Kira burst into thunderous applause and Ted opened his eyes.

Kira really looked thrilled.

„Wow. You really can do it! What was your dream about?“

„That ... That was really beautiful. How long was I gone?“

„Oh ..., maybe a minute. But it looked really intense. What did you dream of?“

„I can't quite remember.“

„Of tonight's concert?“

„Yes. I did.“

„So ... Did it go well?“

„Oh ... it was ... the best concert we ever played.“

Kira smiled happily.

„How was the music?“

„Good. No ... much better than good! It was ... It sounded crisp, yet warm ... it was ...“

„...like a dream.“

„Yes, like a dream. Do you hear and see things clearer in your dreams as well?“

„In my coffee-dreams? Yes. It is a better world. Clearer and more serene, warmer and more relaxed. In the beginning I used to have the image that there was an ocean inside me, with gentle waves, when I moved the coffee back and forth and me and my dreams were on a lilo or in a boat and drifted over wonderfully warm and nicely scented water. During that time I listened a lot to *Ripples* by Genesis – very fitting. You know that song?“

„Yes.“

„Do you want me to put it on?“

27

„No, that's all right. I'm half-expecting *Ripples* to play in my next dream in the background. The ideal song for dreaming ...“

„Oh yes! It always was ... Come, let's dream together!“

Kira sat down in the chair next to the surprised Ted, which was comfortably tight and then both closed their eyes, smelled the pack and took a big sip of coffee ...

Indeed ... *Ripples* was playing ever so softly, but in outstanding quality, in the background, as if Genesis were playing a concert on the beach, while Ted, lying on a lilo, was floating on a lake of crystal-clear water. He looked in the direction of the beach but instead of Genesis, he saw Kira, on a lilo as well, floating slowly towards him. She smiled at him and extended her arms.

For a while they floated across the water hand in hand. The sun was shining nice and warm and the music was soft and playful, like the small ripples on the lake.

Kira had fallen asleep after a while. Ted looked at her relaxed face and her dark hair, in which the sun created infinite shades of black, auburn and gold, fading endlessly into each other and rearranging anew.

Ted pulled Kira's lilo close to his own and leaned over her. He kissed her hair, as if he was trying to drink it. A very long moment on the inside.

Ted lay back down on his lilo, grasped Kira's hand with both of his own ... but just when he noticed that he was about to fall asleep as well, he felt a strong shaking of the lilo. Before he could open his eyes, both of them were carried away by an enormous wave. Softly, warmly but decidedly ...

Ted felt a kiss on his lips. He opened his eyes and saw Kira's face so close to his own, with big hazel eyes watching him in relief:

„Thank God! There you are. For a moment there, I was afraid I had lost you to the dreamworld forever."

Only slowly did Ted return to reality. Just a moment ago he had been far away; far, far away and for a long time ... Had Kira really kissed him just now? Yes, it had quite possibly been the only way to get him back.

„I'm sorry for waking you so rudely from your dream."

„Well, I would hardly call it rudely."

Kira smiled.

„All good then. I would have liked to stay as well but it's about to get busy and I have to get started."

Kira as well looked as if a part of her was miles away.

„I'll make you another coffee, then I'll have to open. You'll find a chair just like this one downstairs; it's empty most times and hardly anybody pays any attention to it, you can go on dreaming there."

„I will. Shall I take you with me, in my dream?"

Kira beamed at him: „Yes, please! That would be nice!"

They went downstairs and Kira showed Ted the chair, standing near the piano. She was on her way to the bar but came back for a moment and gave Ted a long hug.

„In a minute I won't have much time for you anymore and my boyfriend is going to be here in about ten minutes. Anyways, I think you should know that ... That was ..." She could not find the words.

„I think I know what you mean. It was ... something very special. Probably difficult to put in words. It was more like ... music?"

„Yes ... something like that. Perhaps some day you'll write a song about what we just experienced. Anyways ... Don't be sad when I won't have time to talk to you in a moment and smile more at old friends than you."

„No problem. I like little secrets."

„Great."

Kira made him another coffee and opened the Café.

Ted was dreaming away merrily and was amazed at how crowded it had become in the *Kyffhaus Hut* when he opened his eyes again. He must have sunken into the coffee for quite a while.

About thirty people sat at tables inside and outside and had breakfast. Kira's boyfriend, Mirco, too had arrived and helped out behind the bar.

Kira waved at him once but other than that he was now one of many customers, except for the times when she would pass by him and her bright eyes and the scent of her hair would throw him new dreams ...

Just after noon the garage called. The VW bus was up and running again.

Mirco started to describe the way to Ted but Kira interrupted him:

„I'll take the young man to the garage. I have to go into town anyways to do the shopping. Might as well take him with me. Most of the rush has gone by now."

„Okay. See you in a moment."

Ted payed, received the keys and made his way to the parking lot where the VW bus and Kira were waiting for him.

„Well then ..."

They looked at each other a bit sheepishly.

If only the bus would not start!

Or ... - if she would just hop in and come along?

Ted hugged Kira, held her tight and long, because he longed to and he did not want her to see the insecurity in his eyes. Kira returned the hug, at the very least just as tight.

"All the best for your concert tonight and for your continued career as an artist. Play the piano more! And maybe think of me every now and then."

Ted let go of her and looked at her:

"I definitely will! Not only at the piano. With every coffee I will remember last night, your eyes, your hair and our shared dreaming."

Kira blushed, pressed her lips together and looked away for a moment. Then she beamed at him:

"Drink lots of coffee in your life!"

"Absolutely!"

"Wait!"

Kira went to her car, opened the boot and grabbed a bag from it.

"I wasn't quite sure whether ... I have something for you!"

Kira handed Ted the Snoopy cup, from which she had had her coffee yesterday and a large thermos.

"Some coffee for emergencies, should the car break down again somewhere down the road. And my cup, so it's even easier for you to think of me."

Ted beamed at her: "Thank you very much! I will, every time. I'm going to start with it tonight and have a coffee from this very cup at seven o'clock and think of you. It will help me before the concert."

Kira squeezed his hands. „I will have a coffee as well at seven, from your Linus cup and listen to *Homecoming Queen* and cheer for you from afar come eight. All's gonna be well!"

They beamed at each other. Then Kira let go of his hands. Somebody was waving from across the street. Kira looked guiltily at Ted.

„I can't ... Not here ... Maybe you'll come by again ... I will never forget you!"

She hugged him for a long time, then turned around quickly and walked to her car.

A gust of wind blew her long, curly, auburn hair to one side. *Hair, brown like coffee* ... That was it! It did not fit in the song he had already started, also not with Julia, but it was exactly what he had been looking for. He would have to completely rewrite the lyrics. No, actually, he would have to come up with an entirely new song, for piano. He would have to come up with an entirely new self ...

Kira opened her car door and looked back once more. Ted waved and she smiled.

Ted ran to her and they fell into each other's arms once more briefly but passionately and then looked into each other's eyes for a long moment.

„Here!" Kira took off her jacket. „So you won't freeze again on your next hike through the pouring rain. Take care of your-self!"

She kissed his mouth ever so briefly, got into her car quickly, waved once more and drove off.

Ted looked her way for a long time. His face had been covered in her hair during their last embrace and he hoped that the scent of coffee would stick with him forever.

Her hair, brown like coffee and her eyes, at first he had thought of coffee as well but in reality ...

Ted smiled. That dark brown ... That was Madagascar ebony-wood.

Sip Two

The coffee at seven tasted incredible and for a few fleeting moments Ted could actually sense Kira giving him a big hug. He had never been this calm before a concert.

His other bandmates were visibly less relaxed, which lead to a memorable performance that had people in Hamburg talking for years to come, sadly not because of the musical quality.

At the start, their drummer lost one of his sticks, Bernd got a hiccup, which made the quiet parts of the songs sound rather strange and Peter was such a nervous rack that he fell over power chords twice while walking backwards and took the bassist with him the first time around and landed in the drum set on the second occasion.

The audience, who was watching through the first few songs, how horribly this highly praised band performed, had reduced down to half its size before too long, the rest though was starting to have a blast from that moment forward. Every obvious mistake of one of the musicians – and there was no shortage – was met with thunderous cheering; again and again members of the audience toppled over with laughter, taking all sorts of things with them (bystanders, amplifiers, tables) or acted very theatrically as if they too had a hiccup, especially after Peter had fallen down for the third time, which sent his microphone flying into the audience.

„A sign! He gave us a sign! - Follow the microphone!"

„No. Follow the drumstick!"

„Screw the drumstick; follow the sandal!"

Apparently there were quite a few fans of *The Life of Brian* in the audience.

A wild running around broke out in the concert-hall. Most were following the microphone, which they used to sing along loudly and badly or make a hiccup sound.

It was especially bad when the greatest hit of The Flying Dishes was playing: *I'm Falling in Your Arms* – the audience was celebrating this line every time with all of them falling to the ground, which made security and medics who were on duty rather nervous.

The mood in the audience became more and more frisky, while on stage it was falling rapidly below absolute zero. It was actually only Ted, who handed in a decent performance – and as a side note, did not fall over at any point – but when they fled the stage, just short of an hour into their set, it somehow seemed to be all his fault, according to the others.

No dishes actually flew with The Flying Dishes, but two chairs were broken ... and so was the band.

Inside the concert-hall, the party was still going strong and people were screaming for an encore but none of them felt like going out there and making a fool of them again.

While the other bandmembers took refuge in alcohol and drugs, Ted was making coffee.

A little while later, Ted actually took the stage again – not necessarily because of the audience; he had actually hoped, they were gone by now – he simply could not stand being around the rest of the band anymore. Peter became more and more aggressive the more alcohol he had and Bernd, after impressive amounts of cocaine, way too friendly, which was even worse.

Ted also sensed that this would be his last chance for a long while to sit at a piano. He did not have one at home.

But most of all, he hoped to feel close to Kira once more. He had put on her jacket, had his cup of coffee in hand, put it down on top of the piano and played *Homecoming Queen*, not for the few people that were still around, loudly celebrating, but more for a, sadly very far away, darkhaired girl, whose hands he could feel on his own while playing ...

Ted left the last note standing for a long moment ..., that is to say, he would have kept it going on for longer, had it not been for the applause, unlike any other of this evening. Sincere applause.

Almost fifty people were standing in front of the stage, asking for an encore and really meant it.

Ted played a few more songs from the first album on the piano and then remembered his new creation. It already had received new lyrics on the way to Hamburg. The title was clear as well: *Brown As Coffee*. The last verse was sadly still missing though.

Ted had a sip of his coffee, heard Kira's voice „intuitively, the song doesn't want to be written, it wants to be discovered!", smiled and started playing, without knowing, how the song might end.

When he sang the last verse, it felt so familiar to Ted, as if it had been sleeping inside him for a long time. The last line so very fitting, as if there never could have been another:

„You are my favourite kind of coffee."

The Flying Dishes continued – without Ted – but with the last of his money. And they were actually quite successful for a few years. Whereas the attempt to win the crowd over on musical talent alone, completely backfired. Nobody wanted to see serious art. The audience demanded „Fall down! Fall down!" and at some point they did them the favour, completely unnerved and developed over the next weeks a somewhat capable slapstick show, taking a lot from old Laurel and Hardy movies. Literal flying dishes and a microphone wandering through the audience, joined in shortly after.

Ted, on the other hand, was, after paying his debts back to Peter, broke. He really did move back in with his parents.

His old room had by now been transformed into the nail parlour of his mother and all his old furniture had been sold. A bit annoying, but no real harm done. What did hurt though was that they had sold his two guitars as well.

His attempt, to talk his parents into buying a piano as a substitute, ultimately failed – they did not even buy a new guitar.

„I take it, this whole music affair of yours is finally over!", said his father with a triumphant smile and cold eyes.

His plea for a better brand of coffee, than the mild, instant one from Lidl, too failed to convince.

For the first few weeks, they were constantly fighting, very loudly and very angrily; a few months in though, it had become quieter. Ted took this for a good sign, until the silently built up anger exploded during a Saturday evening edition of the sport news, without any forewarning.

Even though Teds snide remark about Bayern Munich had not been the worst thing he had contributed over those past few weeks, it turned out to be the perfect spark to set off the powder keg waiting on inside of his father.

It made for a very loud scene that had the neighbours talking for years to come.

Ted had hated being slapped around as a child; this time he hit back. Which turned out to be an even worse feeling.

Running away from home as well, at the age of twenty-four, was not as cool as it once had been at the age of sixteen.

A roof over his head, central heating and enough food ..., how little he had appreciated those things earlier in his life. Ted stood freezing and with an empty stomach under a bridge and waited for the rain to stop.

In his rucksack, Ted had a lot of the things he considered important: sheets of music, books, Kira's cup and thermos (he was wearing her jacket), but hardly anything of use to him in his current situation, especially warm clothing. For some reason he used to pack a lot more practical when he was sixteen.

And he used to have more money as well. After five nights in cheap lodgings and several futile attempts to find a job, the money had almost completely run out. Should he maybe just swallow his pride, apologise and move back in at home?

But when it came to home, it was not his parents who came to Ted's mind, but Kira.

He hitchhiked his way to Ostfriesland, slept a night in a lorry and was standing, late one evening, in front of the *Kyffhaus Hut* and knocked. His heart seemed to knock as well in his chest.

Sadly it was not Kira, who opened but a young man.

„Sorry, we're closed!"

„Sorry to bother you! Is Kira here by any chance?"

„Kira? I don't know a Kira."

„Her parents own this place, don't they?"

„The owners changed about four weeks ago, and new staff was hired. We don't have a Kira working here."

„Oh ... Pity. Any chance though I could spend the night? I hitchhiked my way here and need a roof over my head."

The man sized him up and Ted realised to his embarrassment that he probably was not exactly looking clean.

„No, sorry. We're fully booked."

Ted took his leave, went a few houses further down the road, waited for all the lights in the *Kyffhaus Hut* to go out and went to the key box. The code was still 4711.

Ted snuck into the house, went to 'her' room, lay down in Kira's bed and quickly fell asleep. He dreamt so intensely and detailed of their night together that it hurt when reality hit him the next morning. But not as much as his ankle, after jumping from the first-floor window, when he had to suddenly flee the room because the cleaning staff had arrived.

Ted freshened up, as far as his meager means allowed him to and went to the *Kyffhaus Hut* again, in the afternoon, to talk to the new owner.

Sadly that one had only heard that the previous owner had moved to the south and the daughter, with her boyfriend, had left the country. He did not know any specifics.

At the very least he allowed Ted to play the piano this evening and in exchange would get a meal and could stay the night.

Playing the piano was wonderful for Ted. The customers were less enthusiastic about it though. Again and again they asked him to play some German Schlager. Eventually an argument broke out over the choice of music that the owner denied Ted to stay the night, gave him a fifty instead and bade him leave the pub.

For a year Ted made his way all around Germany, many times playing the piano in exchange for room and board and just as many times without any engagement, sleeping in shelters or parks.

On a sunny evening in February, Ted was strolling, in Cologne, along the banks of the Rhine and happened to pass the *Café Rheinblick*. He had been refused several times today and was arguing with himself, whether he could still afford another coffee, before trying to find a place for the night.

The *Café Rheinblick* as well offered live music and beds but in a posh place like this, it was usually pointless to even ask. Some retained their professional demeanour, but most let him feel clearly that he did not belong in their world, that his poverty showed.

Ted read the menu in the display on the terrace of the café. The coffee was of great quality but for him unaffordable. He was just turning to leave, when from the inside came the famous cry: „Is there a doctor in the house?!"

Ted grinned. If only he had listened to his father, had finished school, and had studied medicine, instead of forming a band. Ted had only ever done a first aid class, but that one three times, because he had fancied the nurse.

He had practiced first aid on several occasions and had a pretty good idea of what was going on inside: One person was on floor, devoid of any signs of life, while the others were standing in a circle around that person, and just as much devoid of life, hoping desperately that someone would answer their call ...

Ted went into the café. It was a little bit different though this time:

There were quite a few people standing perfectly still around the piano. A young man had fallen unconscious while still sitting on the piano chair; his head rested on the keys of the magnificent, auburn Steinway.

„Please, let me through!"

Ted motioned to a large guy in a suit to lend him a hand and together they laid the unconscious man on the floor, his feet propped up on the chair. Only moments later life returned to him.

Ted felt his pulse – quite irregular and flat. The face was pale and the forehead covered in sweat.

Ted spoke calmingly to the man and issued orders to the bystanders: „Get him some water!" „Grab a blanket!" „And you, get something to rest his head on."

Ted was relieved when finally medics and a real doctor arrived at the scene and took over.

He stood up and looked around. Clean people, expensive clothes, the smell of money in the air; now, with his job done, he felt once more out of place and inferior and yet he had his small triumph:

For a few minutes, he had called the shots, had given instructions to his superiors, without anybody creasing their nose or questioning his authority.

Ted looked around once more, now with more self-confidence, and noticed approving stares; two women were whispering. He had a fairly good idea what they were talking about: „Pretty cool and laid back for a doctor and about your age, Fiona! You should grab him! Best pretend you're fainting ..."

An important looking man made his way directly for Ted, judging by the name tag, the manager.

„Thank you very much, doctor! Excellent job. I'm supposed to know these things as well, from my first aid class but when fate strikes, you're understandably in a bit of shock and you blank, I suppose. But this is your everyday work, isn't it?"

„I'm not a doctor."

„Oh, you haven't graduated yet? Oh well. You are obviously still quite young. It takes a few years of practical experience first, I believe?"

„No. I'm not ..."

„Oh, I thought that mandatory. I think it's better that way. Do you work here, in the hospital?"

„No. I'm not even ..."

„Very reasonable of you! A private practice is a lot more profitable. May I offer you a drink on the house? Never mind that! Have a seat at the bar and order whatever you like. Your tab is on me."

„I ... Oh ... Thank you. Gladly!"

„I'm afraid that I can't offer any live music today though. It's going to be a lot harder to find a substitute piano player than a doctor."

For a moment, Ted was certain the manager would run out onto the terrace and yell: „Is there a piano player in the house?"

But the man stayed where he was and kept going: „While I do love listening to music, I do not play a single instrument."

„I know how to play. Would you mind?"

The manager looked at him in bewilderment.

„Absolutely, my good doctor, oh sorry, not doctor, anyhow: I couldn't possible ask you to!"

„It would be my pleasure. I haven't got a Steinway at home (*under the bridge* – he added in his thoughts) and like to take every opportunity."

„Yes, of course. Gladly! I won't stop you. You really are godsent! I can't pay much though, you know. I'm on a tight budget and ... How much were you thinking about for ... another three hours if you're up for that."

„How much?" Ted's mind was racing; he was not sure, how all this was going to play out, whether or not he would be found out in a moment.

„But of course you won't be playing for nothing!"

„Well ..., I suppose ..., whatever it is you pay the other pianist."

„But ... he's a student! I couldn't possibly, I mean, you being a doctor ..."

„Oh, you know, on the actual instrument we're all pretty much equals. I won't ask for more than your student."

„Are you sure?"

„I am."

„Okay. Fifty euros then per hour, but of course with a free meal and your tab."

„That seems ... perfectly fair."

Ted had several cups of coffee, ate a tuna salad, and played the piano, until the last guest had left.

The manager had stayed as well, gave Ted his money and thanked him once more.

„If you weren't a doctor already, I'd have recommended pursuing a career as a pianist. I enjoyed it very much. Thanks again for saving the evening!"

„My pleasure really! If you haven't found a substitute yet ... I wouldn't mind coming back tomorrow."

„You would ... again? For only 50 euros?"

„The piano sounds beautiful and the tuna salad is the best I ever tasted. Maybe I could ..., well ..."

Ted did not manage to come across nearly as sovereign, as he would have liked for his role of a doctor.

„You know, at the moment, I'm stuck with this dump of a hotel and maybe, for the next week, I could stay here and in exchange play the piano?"

For a moment, Ted was certain, he had overdone it, but the manager beamed at him.

„But of course. We won't be fully booked until easter. Feel free to stay for as long as you like, naturally all-inclusive, plus drinks in the evening and the tuna salad! Deal?"

„Deal."

„Would you like to stay straight away? As I said, we have a few vacant rooms. And you can fetch your luggage tomorrow."

Ted nodded quietly. Had he opened his mouth; he would have been unable to suppress the cheering any longer.

„Brilliant! Have another drink, while I have your room prepared! We have a rather choice whiskey, Glendronach, twenty-five years old, it's ..."

„Thanks. But I'd rather like another coffee; it's really delicious, even though I doubt that it has quite the same age."

„Gladly... Judith! Would you fix another coffee please, for our new pianist?"

The manager excused himself and the waitress put another coffee on the counter, in front of Ted.

„It doesn't have an age whatsoever", she said, laughing „I just put in a fresh pack of coffee beans."

She was about to throw the empty pack in the bin.

„May I see that for a moment?", asked Ted. „The coffee really is excellent; I have to write down what it's called."

She gave him the pack and Ted put it in his rucksack when she was not looking.

A little while later, Ted sat, in the now empty café, smelled the coffee, remembered his nose in Kira's hair, took a sip and moved it around in his mouth.

His dreams had not been this clear and fragrant for a long time.

Ted and Kira were sitting in a boat on their lake and gazed deeply into each other's eyes. Ted had expected *Ripples* to play in the background, instead it was *Chasing Cars* by Snow Patrol, which fitted the moment much better:

All that I am, all that I ever was, is here in your perfect eyes, they're all I can see.

When Gary Lightbody wrote these lines, about the eyes of his girlfriend, had he thought about Madagascar ebony-wood?

The boat was rocking softly, while it kept drifting out onto the lake. Ted rested his head in Kira's lap and gazed into the clear night sky. Between myriads of multicoloured stars, he saw a pretty blue planet.

„Look!"

Kira raised her head.

„Oh, earth. So close tonight. Looks really beautiful from here."

„Do you remember? That's where we met for the first time."

„Yes ..., that was a wonderful night. One I will surely never forget."

„A shame really that we didn't end up together after that night."

Kira nodded.

„Yes, it really is. But at least we have each other here."

„Yes, at least that."

Ted closed his eyes, felt how Kira gently caressed his hair and fell asleep on his hands, the empty pack of coffee next to him on the table, a smile on his face.

Sip Three

Ted sat at the piano, absent-mindedly playing, pondering how things might continue. The manager would have loved to extend his engagement, but the student had a contract and was going to play again, starting tomorrow and so Ted had to find a new job and a new place to stay.

Those five weeks at the *Café Rheinblick* had been wonderful. A room with a view of the cathedral, the sound of the piano, sitting by the Rhine with delicious coffee. But now it was back to sleeping under the bridge and playing on old, discordant, lesser pianos?

He would miss the coffee the most. At noon today, Ted had bought an even bigger thermos and was planning on having it filled to the brim, before he left tomorrow morning.

The song was over. His last break here. Only once more eat here, only one more time a hearty and delicious meal? Ted was neither hungry nor peckish. Instead he got another coffee in his Snoopy-cup and sat down at the bar. With every sip he felt everything calm down inside of him.

Ted grinned – Kira would say: „Something will come up. Life doesn't want to be planned, it wants to be explored! Enjoy your last hour here!"

Ted put on her jacket, took his cup, sat down at the piano, and played, his eyes closed, *Homecoming Queen*.

For the duration of the song, he felt Kira vividly next to him but when he opened his eyes after the last note and looked to his side, he saw, instead of an attractive young brunette, a silver-haired old man with an unkempt beard, beaming at him.

„You are Ted Schäffler, who used to play with *The Flying Dishes*!"

„Yes...?"

Will I be found out not to be a doctor this late in the game?

Luckily the manager was nowhere near at the moment.

„Am I happy to finally have found you!"

The man beamed even more and pulled up a chair next to the piano.

„You played a song during your last concert. The chorus said something about coffee ...?"

„*You are my favourite kind of coffee?*"

Ted sang the chorus.

The man nodded eagerly: „Would you mind playing the whole thing?"

„Not at all."

This time Ted's eyes remained open, but the other man had his eyes closed and seemed to be dreaming.

A full minute after the last note had faded away - Ted had just come to terms with the fact that the man had most likely fallen asleep - he opened his eyes again:

„I've been looking everywhere for this song for so long. Did you never release it, Mr. Schäffler?"

„I ... I have no record-deal at the moment. Actually, for a while now."

„Would you like to record an album with my company? With this song?"

Ted looked at him, puzzled.

„Forgive me! I haven't even introduced myself yet: Harry Record, manager of the label *Everything but the Stars*. Our motto ‚*Music. Not Hits'* is sadly about what you can expect. I can't promise you much in terms of riches, but I'll guarantee you a boss who is bent on good music. Interested?"

Ted nodded.

„Wonderful! I could celebrate with a whiskey. Would you care for a Glendronach as well? It's brilliantly smoky."

„I'd rather have a coffee."

„You are an artist though, are you not?"

„No, mainly I am a simple, barely talented human being, who happened to be kissed once by an exceptional muse."

„Even better!"

Ted said his farewell to the manager of the *Rheinblick*, packed his few things and drove with Harry to Rösrath, where he was shown around the studio and the magnificent old Blüthner-piano with chandeliers and rich adornments.

Ted played a few songs, Harry played two of his own and then they drank wine and whiskey (Harry) and coffee. After brief negotiations, lengthy talks about music and art in general and lots of laughs, they were in agreement:

- Ted had a stage name: Ted Coffee.
- He had a contract for three albums, if possible, within the next six years. A tour was planned after the first album and maybe more if it proved successful.
- Ted got an advance, which allowed him to live carefree and focus on his music.
- And he had a tenancy-agreement at excellent conditions for the house next to the recording studio. It might have been old and in need of renovations but

had all the things important to Ted: An expansive roofed-over terrace, a fire place and a piano in the spacious and well-lit attic, which was suitable as an atelier, due to its many large windows. Additionally he was free to change the garden behind the house to his liking.

Of his first money, Ted bought a few garden-tools and a top-notch coffeemaker.

For an artist, his daily routine was surprisingly well-structured:

After sleeping in, Ted started every day with a cup of coffee, with which he wandered through the garden, looking at what he had created the day before and what had newly grown since.

He enjoyed the sun, the rain or the wind; there hardly was any weather he did not like. Depending on the weather, he either sat down in the garden-swing on the veranda, on one of the benches in the garden or on a tree log.

No matter where he chose to settle down, when he closed his eyes, smelled and tasted the coffee, he was immediately back at the *Kyffhaus Hut* and felt Kira next to him, felt how warmth, joy and music flowed into him, her hands on his own, his nose in her hair, which smelled of music ... and soon he was ready: Music was in all his senses, when he took a sip from her. He saw, felt, smelled, tasted and heard music within himself.

Then he took the coffee and the prepared thermos with him to the piano and attempted to eternalise the muse's kiss in notes.

Within four weeks, Ted had enough songs for his first album.

Harry and Ted had a blast while recording the songs and the album was so successful to allow Harry to book the tour according to Ted's wishes:

Small venues with comfortable seating and dim lighting. Tables and other opportunities to put down a cup of coffee, which was available between songs.

Ted played a few of the old songs on the guitar and a lot of new songs at the piano.

There were many favourable reviews and all twenty-four concerts were sold out.

He neither became very rich, nor very famous but he made enough money to prolong this happiest time of his life up to this point.

He kept composing, at impressive speed, one song after the other, drank vast amounts of coffee and felt his muse close by, every time, unchanged, as if they had met only a short while ago.

That way he completed seven albums within six years.

No doubt, he was happy, happier than he had ever dared to dream and yet, a drop of bitterness always remained:

He so longed to tell his muse, what she had achieved, would have loved to express his gratitude; would have loved to bury his face in her hair once more.

After every new album he went on tour, always hoping that she might turn up at one of his concerts.

Sometimes he regretted, having Harry talk him into adopting the stage name Ted Coffee; maybe Kira had looked for him, but as Ted Schäffler.

He tried to leave her signs. On every record was a rendition of a hit, that described them both, like *Wish You Were Here,*

Ripples, Chasing Cars or *On Every Street*. („It's your face I'm looking for on every street.")

Lyrical homages to the both of them, in the quiet hope that Kira would find him by accident and get it.

He became very clear on the fifth album:

It was called *Street Café* and showed on the cover a photo of the *Kyffhaus Hut*, which by now had been renamed into *Café Nowhere*.

Also on the cover the line from the hit by Icehouse:

No matter where the road may take you
We'll meet again ...Someday at the street café

When he performed those songs at the concerts, he felt Kira so close, as if she was sitting in the audience or could hear him no matter where she was.

Even at home, with a coffee in the garden-swing or during a morning stroll in the garden – sometimes the knowledge that she was thinking of him and the feeling, she was with him.

Then there were times, when he thought it presumptuous. Why should she still remember him after almost ten years? Well, she had promised, not to forget him, but even if she was thinking of him every now and then ... why would he mean anything to her? He could hardly hope to have changed her life as much as she had changed his.

Maybe he was at least a pleasant memory among many others? Every now and then a smile, a pleasant gleaming of a memory, when she had a coffee or played the piano?

Ted drank his last sip of coffee for the day, brushed his teeth and went to bed.

He took the small box of Madagascar ebony-wood, which he had had made last week, from his nightstand, opened the lid, smelled the coffee beans, closed the lid and stared for a long time at the dark-brown texture of the wood, until all he saw was her eyes. The smell of her hair fresh in his nose, he lay back down, cuddled up to her and whispered into her ear:

„You make me very, very happy. I would so love to give you something in return."

The bed rocked slightly, as if it were a boat on the water. Kira put the oars aside and smiled at him:

„But you have, my dear. Do you really believe I would be this present in your dreams if it weren't so?"

Appeased Ted fell asleep.

Sip Four

Ted arrived in Oldenburg, where he was going to play a concert, in the early afternoon. The sun was shining, and he enjoyed a walk through downtown.

As usual, he strolled into *hmv* to check, how many of his CDs they had in stock, what they were priced at and to which other CDs they were next to. Most of the time, Ted Coffee could be found next to Eric Clapton, where he felt the most comfortable. Next to Helene Fischer, David Hasselhoff or even Modern Talking, not so much. He had rearranged his CDs on other shelves before, or if all else had failed, simply had bought them.

He did not find any of his at *WH Smith* but instead the new book by Kimberly Rachel Adams, an Australian author, Harry had been raving about. He finally had the perfect gift for his boss for his sixty-fifth birthday next week!

The check-out was rather crowded, besides Ted disliked buying books in franchise stores anyway. When he would be back home, the day after tomorrow, he would simply buy it at the local bookstore in Rösrath.

Ted strolled through the sun again and had a delicious banana-split in an ice-cream café opposite the mall to cool him down.

On his way back to the hotel, he saw another, rather cosy-looking bookstore – *Bültmann & Gerriets* – with a long line of people waiting outside.

Intrigued Ted came closer and saw a poster hanging in the window: Kimberly Rachel Adams was in town and was signing her new book! With a signature the gift would be even better! Ted got in line.

When he arrived inside the store, a few minutes later, he almost fainted.

Her hair was not quite as dark as it used to be, nor was it as long, but sitting there was definitely not an Australian author, but a born Eastern-Frisian, whose eyes still had the distinctive colour of Madagascar ebony-wood.

Next to her sat two little children and Mirco, maybe; Ted was not quite sure; he had not spent nearly as much time thinking of him over the last years.

It took another five minutes, then it was Ted's turn; in theory enough time to come up with something witty and beautiful, but when he finally faced Kira, no word came out of his mouth, he just put down the book and stared at her in quiet disbelief.

She looked up at him, for the fraction of a second she had beamed at him, he thought, he was not quite sure, no, unlikely, because she was already leaning over the book.

„What would you like me to write?"

„To Ted ... To Ted Schäffler ... Please!"

„Gladly."

She wrote.

She just wrote, without looking up again.

He had said his name, she had heard his voice, but there was no recognition, let alone a long and happy beaming, he so had hoped for.

No. She just wrote and paid him no mind.

Ted's excitement had vanished completely, instead there was now a void inside of him.

Never again would he have that dream, which he had found so many times in packs of coffee and after which he woke up happy:

They met in a chance encounter. She looked at him, recognized him, ran to him with bright eyes and waving coffee-brown hair and flew into his arms so recklessly that they both fell off the lilo.

She had meant everything to him in those last years, had been his drive, inspiration, screw that, his one, his one and only true muse ... - even though he had told his numerous affairs a different story.

What had he meant to her?

Kira had returned the book to him and was taking care of the next person waiting. Ted went outside into the garishly bright sunlight.

All those moments, during concerts or in between, when he had felt that she thought of him in that moment ... *That was just a Dream ...* Maybe he would do a cover of *Losing My Religion* on the next album?

If there was going to be a next album ... Could he even still play the piano, now, without his muse? Did he have to cancel the concert?

Ted went significantly earlier than planned to the concert venue and sat down at the piano. He had intended to play the old songs, but first had the need to somehow express his despair through music. He played with his eyes closed and without him having planned any of it, a whole new song came into being.

A beautiful song, not even melancholic or sad, as he would have expected, rather joyous, but something was ... Ted did not know. He played the song again. He liked it a lot, but ... It was not complete, something was missing. Something essential ... A happily bouncing bird with no wings. The melodies gained momentum ... and then did not take off.

He closed his eyes again and before long, another happily bouncing song came to be.

She kissed like she always had, even now.

Ted grabbed himself a coffee and returned to the piano.

So she still was his muse. That was something he could hold on to. Everything else had been presumptuous.

An hour later he had added four new songs to his repertoire, all without lyrics. The lyrics though were not what was missing.

If it had not been for the first arriving concertgoers, quite possibly Ted would have assembled a whole album over the course of the evening.

It was a strange concert. That he was highly unfocused, went seemingly unnoticed by everybody. As an encore, among others, he played two of the new songs. The audience's reaction was rather subdued, while he had to wipe away a couple of tears.

At the same time, Ted was inspired like never before. He had seen her. She was still unbelievably beautiful. She was still his muse. Just thinking about Kira, led to the spontaneous creation of a completely new song during the concert.

In reality she had forgotten about him, but in the dreamworld of the artists, she seemed closer than ever.

What would have been the difference if she had recognized him? She was married, had children and Ted was seeing somebody as well, albeit not nearly as committed ...

The concert lasted for almost three hours and Ted only returned to his hotel after midnight. He tossed and turned in his bed for a long time. Every time he closed his eyes, he saw her in front of him. This short moment of her magnificent eyes lighting up.

Had there really been such a moment? If she had recognised him, why had she not continued beaming at him, had not said anything? Was her memory of him maybe blurry - *I know him, but from where?* She had most likely known a lot of other people more intimately and more intensely by now. He had been one of many, whose name she could not remember. She did not recall, where they had first met and was embarrassed by that.

When he had finally fallen asleep, he found himself in the same situation in his dream:

Kira sat in *Bültmann & Gerriets*, stood up for every single of her customers, greeted each and every one of them with a hug, a few personal, happy words, laughed merrily and joked around; only when it was Ted's turn, she remained seated, did not look up and asked in a bored fashion:

„What should I write?"

„To Ted Schäffler, please."

She wrote and handed him the book and got up to greet the next customer with a heartfelt hug.

Ted went out onto the street, with hanging head, disappointed ... but most of all, confused: something was weird, something was wrong! He was so consumed by his thoughts that he ran into a display-window and woke up.

Ted sat up in his bed, rubbed his head and stared, half-awake, into the darkness of his hotel room.

There had been something weird indeed, in the real world, which he noticed just now:

„To Ted Schäffler" – it had taken her way too long. Had she written more?

Ted turned on the lights, jumped out of the bed and fell onto the carpet, because his system had trouble keeping up with how important this was to him right now. He crawled over the floor, all the way to his rucksack, took out Kira's book and opened it at page two:

For Ted Schäffler!
P.S.:
The Eau de Cologne is for you ..., in all of my books!

Ted stared confused at her handwriting. *Eau de Cologne?*
He smelled the book but then shook his head:
Nonsense, Ted! She is talking about the key box, but for what? 4711? But ..., what else ..., ah ..., maybe?
He frantically browsed to page 47.
In line 11 it read:
With every coffee I drink, I think of him.
Ted stared at the line in disbelief, pinched himself several times in both arms but it still read the same.

That could not have been a mistake, she had recognised him!

Had she acted so subdued because of her husband and children being present? But ..., really? If so, then not only had she recognised him, then she had ... honestly in every book? He needed all of her other novels right now, urgently, but ..., where to get them now, in the middle of the night?

Ted was close to calling Harry, to ask him if he had all books by Kimberly Rachel Adams and what it said in each of them, on page 47, line 11, but dismissed the thought almost as quickly as the idea to break into *Bültmann & Gerriets* or *WH Smith*.

Instead he drove back to the concert venue, with the vague hope, to gain access to the piano once more. He was lucky indeed. One of the cleaners was just locking up but opened once more for him to get inside, so he could play some more.

She sat down in a chair and enjoyed the free concert by Ted Coffee, all to herself.

Again, it played out of Ted, not songs, only fragments, but before long he realised: There it was, what had been missing with the other four songs, the addition that made sense of all of them.

„Excuse me, do you know how to play the piano?"

The cleaner nodded.

Ted taught her a passage from his first composition and indeed, when she played and he added his new part ... It was a perfect fit ...

Those were not songs for one piano, they were meant for two, for playing together, for two lovers.

Ted hugged the cleaner and returned to his hotel.

Several times more did he read Kira's dedication and line 11; then took a freshly opened pack of coffee and Kira's book to bed with him, rested the book, open at page 47, on his chest and fell asleep shortly after.

When *Bültmann & Gerriets* opened at half past nine, Ted stormed the bookstore, that is, on his inside, on the outside, he could be seen walking briskly yet inconspicuously to the letter A and took all other nine books by Kimberly Rachel Adams to the check-out.

He had a hard time to not immediately check them but for that he would desperately need a coffee. A real coffee and the right environment.

Half an hour later, he sat on his bed, with his steaming Snoopy cup, all ten of Kira's books in front of him, opened them, one after the other and read page 47, line 11:

- *The muse stood in front of my door one night, completely soaked.*
- *I will never forget you!*
- *Without you I wouldn't know my true calling.*
- *I still feel your hand in mine.*
- *Sometimes I wish that I went with you.*
- *Between two waves can lie a whole life sometimes.*
- *Dreams, rich with the scent of coffee, are always good dreams.*
- *No matter where the road may lead you. We will meet again.*
- *In our dreams we have already found each other.*
- *With every coffee I drink, I think of him.*

Ted fixed himself another cup of coffee.

No. He fixed himself **the** cup of coffee. Each of them had tasted of her, the coffees of the last years, all of sweet memory, but this one right here, this one was reality, was here, was now, was her, who obviously still remembered him. No, not remembered, who ... Ted shook his head.

He sat down, with his cup, in a chair, took a long whiff with his eyes closed and had a sip, which he kept in his mouth for a long time.

She had been thinking of him all this time! With every book over the last ten years. He was in her books, like she was in every one of his songs. If only he as well had left such direct and personal messages! At least she seemed to have gotten his cover song ambiguities.

Ted drank his coffee, happily dreaming and shaking his head in disbelief, until he fell asleep in the chair. But even before that, he had lost all ability to discern between dream and reality. On both planes of existence the dreams were exactly the same.

When Ted awoke, a few hours later, in his chair, he felt Kira so vividly next to him like never before. She seemed happy, yet there was something inquisitive in the way she looked at him.

Could it be? Had she herself been just as uncertain as he had been until earlier? Had she similar doubts as to how much she meant to him? He too had not shown any real sign of recognition in the bookstore.

She needed a reply. A coded reply.

Ted drove back to Rösrath, as fast as he could, disappeared in the studio for five days and came out with his next album finished. Of course the four songs for two pianos and then some more compositions, containing messages to Kira.

About possibilities to send her message in code via notes and piano, he had already thought about on his way from Oldenburg back to Rösrath.

Finally, in the studio, he had experimented with several ideas:

The first was the simplest but he disregarded it pretty quickly:

Messages hidden in the lyrics? Too obvious. Plus he felt more like instrumental pieces, rather than actual singing.

He only recorded a cover of *I Though I Lost You.*

So the rest in notes only. But how to write a message with only the letters in an octave at his disposal? The „s" could be played as „es" and counted as well.

Ted started several messages. No, it would not work like that.

If he were to simply follow the alphabet beginning on the low „A" on the keyboard? That would have been better for writing messages but sounded horrible. He had to compromise somewhere.

Maybe text in every 11th and 47th stave, or every 47th note a letter, or note 11 and 47?

Ted tried everything, until he found a working mix of all of them plus a fill-in-the-blanks text, which could just be deciphered, and at the same time did not sound too bad.

On the album cover, Ted's piano from his attic could be seen. On it was a bottle of Eau de Cologne and several books by K.R. Adams. Some of the keys had letters on them, as hints to parts of the encryption.

Name of the album: *The Code*

Sip Five

„And the winner is ..."

Ted had dreamed of this moment for weeks since he had been nominated for an Oscar for the best original score, and then had heard his name at this moment ...

But now he was happy not to be the winner.

He had suffered from terrible stage-fright all day, had not eaten anything, and had hardly spoken a word when someone had addressed him.

And just now he had felt clearly that he would have fainted, had Julia Roberts called out his name.

No, it was better that way ..., not to mention the fact that the score by John Powell was genius and had rightfully won.

Ted had no reason to complain anyway.

The nomination of his album alone had doubled record sales over the last weeks.

Kira had been famous for years now, especially since her second book (*If You Had Stayed*) had been adapted for the screen very successfully.

Now, as an influential and well-known author, she had had her say when it came to the cast and the score and had recommended Ted Coffee.

And Kira had indeed won the Oscar for the best original screenplay. When her name had been announced as the winner, she had jumped out of her seat and had spontaneously hugged Ted before everybody else, who was seated behind her.

Even an Oscar of his own could have hardly felt this good.

More excited even than Ted, were the program directors of Pro7. Having six Germans nominated in various categories was a first and three of them had actually won.

There had been several special programs before the actual live broadcast, which had been extended to fifteen hours and afterwards a special talk with all six nominees was spontaneously set up.

Ted would have liked to skip the last, but Kira had told him with bright eyes: „See you in a moment!" that he could not bring himself not to do it.

It was her day and Ted did not want to ruin it.

When he sat on stage though, a short while later, he dearly regretted having been so considerate.

Ted had ample time to fully enjoy his anxiety and to perfect it. Before him, three other nominees in the group were interviewed.

The first was witty and funny.

The second so gorgeous that everybody would have been at her feet, even if all she would have done were to smile and say nothing; it did not help him in any way that she was also very smart and well-read.

And the third was an author of short movies, who did not only win the Oscar but also had an extremely cool voice.

Ted was shaking on the inside and the sweat was running down his back. Without a piano in front of him, he felt naked and insecure.

While he had prepared a few anecdotes and replies for likely questions, now that he was sitting on stage, with everything rolling towards him, he felt just like he did back in *Bültmann & Gerriets*:

He had forgotten everything and would most likely be unable to say anything in a moment.

Also, it was in no way helpful that the host kept mentioning over and over again, how many million people from around the globe were watching.

The short movie author had finished, and Ted fell backwards off his chair, at least mentally. In the outside world, he could keep an upright position by desperately clinging to the armrests.

„Mr ..., er, Coffee? That's not really your name, is it?"

Ted really had to think hard about it and was unable to remember his real name because of all the excitement.

„I ... Just call me Ted."

„Okay ... Ted! Many critics have tried and failed to pinpoint the special element in your music. Could you yourself maybe give us an idea?"

Yes, he had expected a question like that. But what was the correct answer again? Ted stared, desperate for help, to the piano, which was standing next to the stage. Luckily, the booming silence was interrupted by the animation specialist:

„Could we maybe get something other than water and juice? We have reason to celebrate after all!"

„Of course, what would you like?"

„I would say, Champagne for everybody would suit the occasion! I know, you are on a tight budget ... It'll be my treat!"

The host turned to the directors:

„Could you get some Champagne, please? The good one! Mr. Wedell is paying!"

„No problem."

Kira raised her hand: „To be honest, I don't really like Champagne. Would it be possible to get a coffee?"

Ted nodded in relief: „Oh, yes. For me as well, please!"

„Four bubblies and two coffees then?"

All nodded in agreement.

While the drinks were being procured, there was a short commercial break, then a visibly flustered assistant director came to the group, handed out the Champagne and placed a cup of black coffee in front of Kira; milk and sugar stood at the ready on a tray.

„How do you take your coffee, Miss Adams?"

Ted smiled: „With lots of milk, a teaspoon of sugar and please unstirred."

„You know that so well?", asked the host in amazement.

„I read all of her books. It's the way the heroine always drinks it."

Kira nodded, beaming. „That's the way I love my readers! For Ted, almost black, please. With just a spot of milk."

„I take it, you know this one from a song?"

„Yes, from *My Hot Little Black*."

Ted felt a lot better with a cup in his hands. After every question, he would first take a sip and while moving the coffee around in his mouth, the words would come to him.

„So, Ted. Again: Many critics have tried and failed to pinpoint the special ingredient in your music. You have a rhythm that is unmistakeably yours. Can you maybe explain it yourself?"

„Not really in all its details, but since you are the first to ask me this important question, I will share with you that part of the truth that I have grasped: The secret of my music are the pauses; when my music isn't there that's when the rhythm comes into being. This is also true for the rest of my life. What makes me, what gives me momentum and rhythm, what makes me dance, is something that isn't even there, someone, who ... ... you ..."

Ted noticed to his surprise that he was no longer focused on the host but was looking directly at Kira.

A moment later, he also noticed that his voice had trailed off even though he had never finished his sentence.

„Ted?! Are you still with us?"

The host seemed honestly worried. And Kira as well looked at him sternly; *Don't screw this up – I know all of it already!*

„I'm sorry. I was distracted for a moment ... Where was I?"

For the next questions, he refrained from looking at Kira, which did much for his ability to focus.

When Ted, for the fifth time now, took a sip before answering another question, the host smiled:

„Well, by now I am convinced that your name really is Coffee."

The host focused his attention on Kira now. About time too – Ted's cup was empty.

„Congratulations on your Oscar, Miss Adams! Or may I call you Lady Kira?"

„Thank you. Yes, of course."

„After hearing some of what makes the mystery surrounding Ted Coffee's unique style ... What is the secret behind your books, Lady Kira?"

„There is actually a bit of a similarity to be found to Ted Coffee. The people, who are the focus of my stories, are, for the most part, not real or at least not visible for most and what I am trying to say in my work, lies somewhere, inaudible and invisible, between the lines."

„Speaking of inaudible and invisible. You came to fame through your crime-series 'James', which is soon to be turned into a movie. Heroine of your story is a young Lady named Kira, who lives in a castle and solves crimes. Helping her is the, to all but her, invisible butler James, who gives her crucial clues, protects her from danger and ..."

„...helps around the house and everyday things – that is an important trait for a real hero!", interrupted Kira.

„Yes. No doubt about it. He makes coffee, lights the fire-place, plays the guitar and the piano for her, is always there, when the lady needs him and yet ... something is very elusive about him. He never speaks a word, is invisible to everyone else. He has something of a ghost ... Has the character been influenced by a father, gone too soon?"

Kira shook her head with a smile.

„As an author, you should never allow people to pick your brain too much, it is restrictive. No, who was inspiration for which character, I will give away just as little, as I would the identity of a muse. Just this: My father has absolutely nothing to do with James, but it is true that the person I think of, when writing this character, is mainly found outside my real life."

„Miss Kira, the lady is a self-confessed coffee afficionado and expert but always has her coffee in the same exact spot and all by herself, always from the same cup, always the same brand, with the same amount of milk and sugar. How do you feel about newer variations, like *Latte Macchiato*? Or maybe a *coffee to go*, so that the lady can have her coffee while strolling through the castle gardens; after all, it is where she has her best ideas, isn't it?"

„Oh, I love *coffee to go*. Although I have a different under-standing of it than you. I make a mixtape with the music of Ted Coffee and play it on my Walkman, while hiking through the mountains or walk along the river. Indeed, it is where I have great ideas. The lady remains in her armchair in front of the fireplace. It is possible that it is not the coffee alone that gives her the ideas ..."

„...but the bearer of the coffee also brings the ideas?"

„Rather inspires the ideas."

„Luckily, we have another expert here with us in the audience ... Miss Adams Junior, how does your mother take her coffee at home?"

Kira's daughter shrugged:

„Actually, we don't really know for sure as well. Most of the times, she has her coffee in her study, where not even the rest of the family is allowed in. But she actually has a *coffee to go*. First thing every morning, she fixes herself a coffee and goes for a stroll through the garden. Always all by herself."

Kira smiled. „I'm not really alone there. Somebody always walks with me, invisible for everybody but me. It is the time of the day when James mostly appears to me ... And of course at seven in the evening."

„Are we ever going to hear James talk?"

„I won't rule it out. I'm not planning on it, but my characters rarely ever do what I expect them to and evolve in surprising directions, while I write. Besides that: James does talk to me, maybe not in words, but in books, which he lays out for me but most of all with music, on the piano or the guitar ... He speaks in a melodious and touching manner with me, in a language without words that warms my soul when I feel cold and heals when I fell sick ... Granted: Sometimes I have the feeling, he's trying to tell me something specific when playing the piano, as if he was trying to play words ... But so far, I have been unable to make sense of it. Words may be my area of expertise but not the translation of piano music ... Maybe Ted Coffee knows more about it. He is not unlike James; the silent type ... I think, you too would prefer to answer through the piano rather than words."

Ted nodded and the host followed up:

„What would you say to the lady if only you could speak through the piano?"

Ted went to the piano and played the chorus of one of the compositions of his last album.

The host looked at Ted, puzzled: „And exactly what did you just tell the lady?"

„I will be there when you need me."

„Okay ... I wouldn't have made that out immediately. Is there some sort of translator for it?"

„Yes, the album-cover", said Kira, while she eagerly wrote something on a napkin.

Ted smiled and nodded. The host looked in confusion at both of them.

"The last album, before your latest, was called *The Code* and showed a piano with letters on the keys, on the cover", Kira explained, without looking up from her writing.

„You are playing letters, Ted?"

„It's not that simple, actually. Would I be playing this sentence according to letters alone, it would sound like this:"

Ted again played something on the piano, and it sounded horrible and nothing at all like the song he had just played. He smiled:

„The code isn't easily deciphered ..., but there are two people in the world I trust to do so: Benedict Cumberbatch and Lady Kira."

„Yes ..., exactly ..., the lady ..." The host turned once more to Kira. „What are you writing down anyway? Napkins reportedly have a reputation for delivering the best stories about wizards."

„No, I am trying to solve the code. Actually, I have been for a long time, but today is the first day, where I am really making progress. Could you say another sentence and play it too, Ted?"

„Gladly: *I'm happy that you exist!*"

This time, Ted played something from his instrumental compositions on the piano and Kira took further notes.

The host could not help but feel that he was losing his hold on the conversation and pulled his ace from up his sleeve.

„While you're at the piano, Mr. Coffee ..."

Ted had expected, to be asked, to play the song he had been nominated for, but the host had a real surprise in store for him and even more so for Kira.

"...and may I ask you as well, Miss Adams!"

The curtain behind Ted's piano was lifted and revealed a light-brown Steinway.

„After all, we too have read the books; maybe not all of them and not as thorough as Ted Coffee maybe, but the light-brown Steinway, at which James sits and plays to the lady, was mentioned enough times and described. And ... We know, not entirely by coincidence ..." He gave a quick glance in the direction of Kira's daughter „....that you know how to play the songs for two pianos, Lady Kira. You may choose, which one you would like to play together with Ted Coffee."

Kira looked baffled and hesitated before she stood up; she had to steady herself momentarily. Ted too had stood up and walked towards her. They looked at each other uncertainly; then smiled, took of their microphones, stepped aside, and had a quick heart-to-heart. The fact that he felt and could smell Kira's hair did no favours to his already weak knees.

„I think I'm going to be sick from all this excitement", whispered Kira.

„Don't be afraid. I'm going to make a bigger fool of myself, than you ever could. Nobody expects of me to choke, when sitting at the piano. I played this song so many times and dreamed of you playing at the other piano: but I was never this nervous, like now, with you really sitting there."

„I had a similar dream, so many times. Actually, the same dream." Kira beamed at him now completely overjoyed. „This is our shared dream and now it finally becomes reality ... Let's enjoy it!"

„Yes! Absolutely! We take our coffees, raise our cups to each other, say a magic spell and all other people will disappear and only we will be left ..., finally just the two of us ..."

Kira briefly squeezed his hand; then they returned to the stage and had their cups refilled.

„James ..., if you please?"

Ted bowed, took Kira by the hand, lead her to her piano and afterwards went to his own. When they both were seated, they raised their cups to each other and slowly took a big sip.

There was no need for a spell, everything around them disappeared and they played, dreamed and enjoyed together ...

The phonelines at Pro7 were burning up; many viewers complained about the picture being out of focus; or rather Ted and Kira, to be exact, while the pianos, coffee cups and the audience were perfectly in focus, when the camera panned.

A technician was consulted after the broadcast and explained the whole thing with a power spike, which had caused a temporary malfunction in the camera's autofocus.

What he was not asked and what he would have been unable to explain anyway was:

The audience in the studio as well was rubbing their eyes, because they could only make out Kira and Ted's silhouettes, as if phantoms had taken their seats, transparent husks, as if they were here as a reflection only and in reality somewhere else entirely ...

At some point, someone came up with the idea that behind all this was the sixth nominee of the evening. He had, after all, received the Oscar for the best visual effects. Maybe a trick with the lights.

The explanation went viral among the audience, leading to everybody taking to listening and enjoying once more, completely at ease. There was no way that Kira and Ted had really gone after all. They were unmistakeably there. They played beautifully; all four songs for two pianos, one after the other ...

Sip Six

Ted's following albums were surprisingly happy. The critics were raving and wrote, he had reinvented himself. The sales too went up considerably.

Ted could have filled big halls or small stadiums, but he insisted, like before, to play small venues with a maximum capacity of a thousand viewers, furnished with tables with candles on them, bars with stools, sofas and comfortable armchairs. The small breaks too, allowing people to get more coffee, remained part of the program.

Internationally he was in high demand as well. Six months of touring through the United States, Australia and all of Europe. An exciting time for Ted, who had not seen much of the world before that.

Ted was approached by several big coffee producers and offered lucrative deals, which he all turned down. Instead he gave several private concerts at a small coffee plantation on the hills of the Kilimanjaro.

Many artists wanted to play a duet with Ted. He turned down most of them; with Mark Knopfler however, he went on tour for three weeks – with an extra long version of *On Every Street* playing during every concert.

After the tour, he focused on an entirely different project:

He bought the former *Kyffhaus Hut*, which had been vacant for several years and had fallen into disrepair. It was restored, as much as possible, to its former self and reopened as the „*Street-Café*".

The interior and atmosphere resembling a mix of Viennese coffeehouse and Irish pub. The music heavy on the piano.

There were no prices for the meals on the menu. The customers were asked to pay what they thought it was worth and those who could not pay anything, received a free meal and if need be, a night's accommodation, including a shower in the morning, a cup of coffee with breakfast and a thermos to take with them.

On occasion the manager himself would play an impromptu concert at the *Street-Café*.

Other than that, everyone was free to play the piano, who treated it respectfully; Wednesday afternoon had free piano lessons for children.

In the meantime, Harry had expanded his record label with a publishing branch and his mostly unknown authors would hold readings there and some of them actually made it to fame.

Another, for a long time now, very well-known author published her next book shortly after Ted's album. On page 47, line 11 was as a phrase, Ted had played in code on his last album:

When souls resonate in shared music, distance is of no consequence.

Kira had cracked the code.

She too wrote more books than before. And additionally she started publishing in a blog, in the guise of *Kira Raki*, in irregular intervals „*Letters to James"*.

Ted had never played by notes at his concerts, the thingy, meant for holding the sheet music on his piano, had always remained empty; now, several pieces of paper were propped up there. It still were not any notes but rather the newest letters to James.

That way he felt even more comfortable at the piano, felt Kira even closer and the already long concerts now usually went on until midnight.

During a concert in Hamburg it finally happened:

Ted had played for five hours already, had felt something resembling a tinge of fatigue for quite a while now, but the roundabout five hundred people in the audience kept demanding encores, even though he had already said his final goodbye and had left the stage for a third time. The venue was brimming, quite possibly nobody had left so far.

Ted stood in the room behind the stage, had a sip of coffee and read the newest *Letter to James* one more time, which he had discovered and printed out just before the concert.

You are the little book on my nightstand, in which I read, before I fall asleep and then dream beautifully;

in which I read a page in the morning and head in the new day, a spring in my step.

The booklet in my pocket, through which I browse, when I take a break during the day and sit in the sun.

The little treasure between the myriads of tomes in the library, I browse, am fascinated, sit down on a bench and disappear into larger, better, distant worlds and forget all the other books around me, the people around me, my past, my future ... only this unique book, with the story, in which I find everything, I always longed to be, what I still long to be.

The book I rest my hand upon, when I take an oath; where I want to rest my weary head, when I return home, tired from the day.

The third thing I would take with me on a deserted island, next to notepad and a large pot of coffee.

The book of our beautiful friendship!

Carefully I close the book, caress its cover tenderly once more and press you to my heart. Tomorrow I will read on.

Ted smiled happily. He suddenly felt in the mood for a never-ending party. It did not matter whether he felt close to Kira in bed or at the piano. So he went back on stage.

„Okay, you asked for it. I said many times, I could play my favourite piece for all eternity. I haven't tried that so far ... Let's see who can go on longer, you or me!"

Ted sat back down at the piano, with a newly filled thermos and his Snoopy-cup and played *Coffee For One* for five hours,

Just after six in the morning, there were still more than three hundred people left; physically exhausted but happy.

The only downer: The venue had run out of coffee.

Ted went, with almost two hundred fans into a café in the city, which had just opened and at this hour usually had no more than ten customers.

Artist and audience were so equally touched that Ted returned the next year and extended another concert into breakfast.

The café in the inner city added three additional staff for that morning.

The ritual was refined over the next years: The audience brought roll mats and blankets, some came in costumes, e.g. as a patient with coffee on an I.V. Pole.

A few other cities joined in as well, if the audience had 'earned' a night-concert and a fitting *Letter to James* had been published:

A few days ago, a critic called me the „most fertile goddess of the modern day", because I had created so many new worlds.

I found the comparison quite unfitting and horribly exaggerated, but these days I like the thought, because it allows me to express, just how wonderful you are:

If ever you should doubt yourself, think of this:

Who is greater than a goddess? He, who breathes life into the goddess and her creative genius, with his kiss.

A goddess had been your student.
You taught a goddess how to fly.

Sip Seven

Five hundred people, in high spirit, drank, laughed and stood in groups together. Ted sat alone on his small table, drank his coffee and regarded with little interest, what was happening around him. He had never felt comfortable in large crowds if it was not a concert.

It was not his world and yet she, who he was here for and who was just now dancing with her husband on the big stage, was so much more of a world to him, than reality had ever been.

Kira looked at him and waved in his direction with bright eyes, he smiled and raised his cup to her.

It was nice to see her again after all those years, but until now they had not had a single minute for just the two of them.

At least the speeches were over! All afternoon countless important and famous people had said a few things in Kira's honours and had congratulated her.

Kira, just like Ted, usually did not care for large festivities, but with the special constellations in this year, she had finally caved under the pleas of her publisher, as he mentioned proudly in his speech.

„I know, dearest Kimberly, that you would rather celebrate by yourself with your butler near the fireplace but this time I won over James ..., at least this one time! Your 47th novel has been published today and you have sold over 47 million copies. Had it been up to me, we would have celebrated two weeks ago:

Your 47th birthday seemed a perfect fit, but sadly the book hadn't been finished by then."

Kira grabbed a microphone:

„Oh, Gustav. You actually won double. Not only did I agree to your party; the fact that it is today is not a coincidence ... You are a born and proud citizen of Cologne and user of Eau de Cologne, aren't you? Today I am 47 years and 11 days old, I have sold 47.11 million books and have published 47 books and finished 11 chapters of my next project ... There couldn't have been a better date for this party."

The audience applauded, Kira's boss beamed and continued with new energy into an even longer speech.

Ted was the only celebrity at the party, who had not held a speech, but had played something on the piano for the honouree. As thanks, he had received a very long and very warm hug from Kira, which he would have liked to have enjoyed without all the people around him ..., but still:

Even though they had hardly spoken, even though Ted hated travelling by plane, especially twenty hours to Australia ...

It had been worth it!

He would feel the hug for a long time to come, the image before his inner eye had been updated. Her hair was by now light brown to grey, but her face was, thanks to all the laughter lines, even more beautiful than ever before and that gleaming in her eyes of Madagascar ebony-wood ...

Ted felt a great longing to sit down at the piano in the corner and to relieve some pressure from this rumbling volcano of inspiration, he could feel inside.

But the piano was covered, several glasses on top of it, an ashtray, with someone just now flicking his cigarette in it, while talking to someone.

Ted's coffee-cup was empty, the staff was busy, and Kira was taken away once more for photos and talks with the press.

Ted waited a while longer, dreamed of sitting at the piano with Kira but another ten minutes passed and no one came by with whom he could order another coffee, he left unseen, and quite happy about that, the room.

During the speeches over the course of the day, Ted had become so tired that he had nodded off several times; now that he finally was in bed, long after midnight, he was wide awake.

Somewhere in this building, Kira was asleep; a thought that did not do anything in terms of making Ted sleepy.

Instead he noticed a strong craving for a coffee. Maybe by now the hotel bar would be a little less crowded.

Indeed, where just a while ago a few hundred people had been, only seven people remained. Quiet music, subdued conversations.

Ted had a seat at the bar and ordered a large cup of coffee with a spot of milk.

As always he closed his eyes and enjoyed the wonderful scent of her hair in his nose, only to then dip his mouth into her curls and briefly kiss the coffee, before keeping the first, very hot sip in his mouth for a long time and then, directing much of its warmth to his heart, let it run down his throat ...

In that fashion, Ted emptied the cup in seven sips, before opening his eyes again.

He had almost expected to see Kira in front of him, he felt her so close; instead a dark-haired waitress, by the name of Katja, stood in front of him.

„Only once before in my life have I seen someone drink a coffee like this ... - if one can all it drinking at this point."

She had a big grin on her face.

„I've worked in service for many years now, but have never seen anything like this, until now! And both on the same evening ..."

Ted looked at her baffled. „This evening?"

„Yes. Half an hour ago, I reckon. She took a pot of coffee and I think she mumbled something about a nice view from the roof, on a clear night with a full moon."

„On the roof?"

"Yes. I told her about the roof-terrace of our hotel when she asked for a quiet place. Hardly anybody knows about it. The lift only goes up to the twelfth floor and from there you would have to take the small narrow stairs, next to the bathroom, up another two levels. You basically have the whole place to yourself at any time. I like to sit there as well every now and then after my shift is done. I won't tonight though. I wouldn't want to disturb anybody ..."

She winked at Ted.

„But ..., how did you know?"

„I have read all Lady Kira novels and have seen the eyes of Miss Adams, when someone was talking about Ted Coffee at the table. Service staff may not always entirely be made up of intellectuals, but when it comes to relationships and unfulfilled dreams, we are second to none ..."

Ted stared at her.

„Don't worry. I don't think anybody else had noticed. Her husband hadn't been with her. Would you like to take a pot as well?"

Ted beamed at her: „Two, if possible. I think James would have brought her one as well."

„Absolutely!" The waitress beamed as well.

With two pots of coffee and some biscuits on a tray, Ted made his way to the rooftop-terrace.

Kira turned around when she heard the door creak behind her and beamed at Ted.

„Had I written this scene, I would have most likely cut it again, because it would have seemed to unlikely to me ... Hello, James!"

„Madam ... If you do not mind, I won't remain silent for to-night."

„But of course!"

That being said, for a long time no one said a word. After a long and heartfelt hug, they now just beamed at each other and drank coffee ...

After the second sip, Kira briefly caressed Ted's arms and rested her hands on his.

„I just had to make sure that you are really here. It is so sur-real, as if I had just woken up in one of my books ... Even though it feels very familiar, being alone with you, drinking coffee. It is pretty much like every day, but somehow com-pletely different."

„Honestly, every day?"

„Sometimes more, sometimes less intense, but yes, every day ... Thank god, you didn't kiss me as my muse every day. It had been a rather busy life thanks to you already."

Kira let go of his hands and amicably punched Ted in the shoulder.

„Forty-seven books have I published, thanks to your kisses and roughly another two hundred fifty unfinished ones are still in my head ... Will you ever be satisfied?"

„What am I supposed to say? Twenty-four albums ... There is hardly a more diligent musician out there, or so they say. But it wasn't really me after all. Will you ever stop kissing?"

„Do you want me to?"

„For heaven's sake, no! Never!"

„Me neither."

They raised their cups to each other, but before they actually drank, they hugged each other one more time, very long and very tenderly ...

„You wouldn't believe how much I was looking forward to this party, not because of all the celebrating because of the various anniversaries ... No, our party ..., right now."

„You mean ... You thought about it as well?"

„Oh Ted ..., of course! My book had been finished at the beginning of this year; I just didn't tell anybody. I simply didn't want to celebrate on my actual birthday. My publisher had been so dead wrong! James had, as always, clearly won. I never wanted to hugely celebrate anything, but when he insisted, I thought: If I have to, it's going to be with you at least, on our twenty-fifth anniversary ... I'm sorry that you had to sit through all the festivities. I had noticed that your cup was empty and would have loved to bring you a fresh one, but that would have been too obvious ..."

„I would have liked to sit with you at the piano ..."

„Speaking of piano ... I've become rather good at your code, most times listening is enough now to decipher it. I was very touched by what you had sung this afternoon about our first evening ..."

„I didn't sing."

„Oh ..." Kira laughed. „Right. For everyone else it was purely instrumental ... I think it's better anyway that only I got the lyrics ..."

„Yes. No doubt."

„It had really felt to me like a song, I clearly heard your voice inside me, whenever I had understood the notes right away ... But what I meant to ask: In the song my name came up several times, always in the same way, only at the end it was somehow different ... Is there any meaning to this?"

Ted blushed and Kira smiled:

„I knew it ... Could it be that my first name was still the same, but now I had a different surname?"

Ted nodded, still unable to say anything. That she could read him so precisely ..., he had not expected that.

„If my ears didn't deceive me, after my first name now came the notes es, c, h, a, e, f twice and again e... Kira Schäffler...?"

Ted nodded and simultaneously shrugged his shoulders apologetically: „Just a little allusion that it might have been an entirely different song ..."

„...that life could have been different entirely?"

Ted nodded.

Kira looked at him with deep dark eyes and hugged him long and warm. Her arms stayed around him when she backed off to talk to him.

„Thank you for the song. It means a lot to me that for a line I had your name ..."

„Oh, Kira ... What would have become of us if you had come with me, back then? Do you dream of it too, sometimes, what might have happened if we had lived together?"

„Sometimes? Well ... Twenty-five years together, having sex and children with you, a tempting idea and a very frequent and always pleasant dream. But I'm afraid, a lot of art would have been lost on the world if we had been together. We only would have drunk coffee together all the time, played the piano, cuddled, dreamed and made cute little babies. Writing and composing would have been impossible, timewise. Besides: Unfulfilled wishes, unsatiated desires and the hopeless longing for the beloved person, that is the motivation behind our art. Bukowski put it so fittingly: 'Writers are desperate people and when they stop being desperate, they stop being writers.' You are the most magnificent despair I can imagine for myself. And you know that I am good at imagining wonderful things. No. We have done everything right. There is no doubt in my mind that we would have been happy together, but we possibly ended up even better: We actually are happy the way it is. We gave each other a full life, filled with overflowing fantasy and creativity; we carried each other through tough times, without physically touching each other. And in a way, we have lived together: I was with you on stage every evening, in every song of yours and you were in all of my books. It was the most ingenious life I have ever heard of. Happy in the real world and overjoyed in our dreams."

Ted nodded in silence. He would have liked to play her his response on the piano, felt clearly that there were at least seven new songs in him, but now was not the right moment for that. Even she, queen of all words, fell silent for a long while and only beamed at him happily, before resting her head against him.

They drank coffee and overlooked the city in silence. Only after her next sip, several minutes later, did Kira raise her head again from Ted's shoulder:

83

„Twenty-five years ago, we met. Since then, I have dreamed so many times of being alone with you and to tell you everything. I have had hour-long talks with you, in my mind, in which I bared my heart to you ... What is inside myself for you, is immeasurable! But now words fail me. Me, who has made a living of finding nice ways to put things, these words ...“

Ted put a finger on her lips. She sighed in relief and whispered:

„Thank you!“

Ted smiled:

„What does it say in Werther: 'I couldn't paint right now, not a single stroke, and have never been a greater painter.' - You have no words, I have no notes ... Right now it would be impossible for me to play the piano, even though I have always played only for you.“

They fell silent for a while and beamed at each other.

„I was so distracted a moment ago that I didn't pay attention: Does your hair still smell of coffee?“

Kira smiled and bowed her head. Ted finally buried his face once more in her hair and wanted to instinctively take a sip, but her hair in his mouth brought him back to reality, which was today, for a change, even more beautiful than all of his dreams.

The coffee in his cup had been cold for a while now, but the coffee in his arms had just the right temperature and tasted delicious ...

Sip Eight

For the twenty-fifth anniversary of the Street-Café, Kimberly Rachel Adams had been announced as the guest of honour and was going to read some of her work.

Ted had tried for weeks, to fix a decent tuna-salad and had finally found a recipe, which made his desert come somewhat close to the best tiramisu from, by now, forty-five years ago.

But ten days before her planned appearance, Ted received a phone call from Kira's manager; he had to cancel, since Kira had taken ill. He would not go into any further details, even after being asked to do so several times.

Ted knew that it had to be something serious, otherwise Kira would not have cancelled or at the very least, would have spoken to him directly. They both had been looking forward to seeing each other again in their old place.

Two weeks later, Ted sat in a café, had a coffee, and read in the newspaper that Kimberly Rachel Adams had passed away.

His heart stopped, thought better of it, and continued beating, rather listlessly.

Ted fell of his chair and was brought to the hospital.

The head physician of the clinic explained to him that he had cardiac dysrhythmia, bigeminy, to be precise. Every other heartbeat was to weak and did not pump enough blood.

„Yes. I half-expected something like that. I know that from before, it happened to me with some compositions. Half of it wasn't properly working there as well ... or at least the essential bits. I got it working again in the end. But this ... My heart will remain broken."

„No. The heart isn't broken; it is only a dysfunction of the impulse conduction."

„I wouldn't put it like that."

„It can be treated in any case."

„No. I'm afraid not."

„Yes. There is a drug for it."

„The remedy that could help me has been taken of the market a few days ago ..."

„Nonsense! There is something even better by now! Take the prescription I give you, in the morning and in the evening and you'll see: good as new!"

„You really have no ideas of matters of the heart!"

The head physician, quite excited about the fact that he was treating such a famous patient, finally managed to convince Ted to be treated for his cardiac dysrhythmia in-house.

In the evening, after trying a sip of the coffee served in the hospital, Ted decided to leave, much against the doctor's recommendation, and went home.

No, he would not let anybody get near his heart. Somewhat curious though that only every second heartbeat fell short. Ted did not really have the feeling to still be alive. Everything that used to fulfil him, now only left him more hollow.

He sat at the piano, the sounds and songs sounded strange to him; he could not read Kira's books. The lady was silent, and James stood next to her, clueless ...

Everything that would have normally helped, failed, the coffee at home too tasted bland.

Ted cancelled all concerts; the Street-Café remained closed until further notice.

Two days later, mail arrived from Australia: In a large envelope were the letters of a notary, a plane ticket and another, smaller sealed envelope. Ted read the notary's letter first:

He was mentioned in the testament and was asked to please, if at all possible, be present, when it was opened. All expenses, travel and otherwise, had been paid for by Miss Adams, preemptively. Apparently it was important to her for him to be there.

Ted opened the smaller envelope, saw the familiar and much-loved handwriting and fixed himself a coffee, before reading the letter.

My beloved friend,

nothing in my life was ever so hard to write like this letter.
(And I am not talking about my weak, twisted fingers ...)

I know that you are feeling poorly at this moment, that you do not like flying and only want to be left alone, but I want to ask my second-to-last favour of you:

Be there when they open my will! It is of the utmost importance to me that only you receive, what I have left you. Additionally, I hope to be with you a little while longer, just once more, because I have everything ready for you.

It is also very important to me that you meet my youngest daughter Julia.

I am not sure, whether this letter reaches you unopened, but that, which I would have written otherwise, James knows, even without words ...

I have written millions of lines during my lifetime, the last of which to the person responsible for said millions ...

I am uncertain as to where I am off to now, but I am sure that there will be excellent coffee and we will enjoy it together again soon.

Yours,

Kira

Ted drank, with his eyes closed, a delicious sip of coffee and noticed at the same moment that his heart was beating calmly and evenly again.

It had not been her part in his heart that had been missing. He himself had stopped and she had kept beating on inside of him, to keep him alive ...

Eleven people were present at the opening of the will. Ted, the notary, her publisher, Mirco and several of her children and grandchildren.

Ted sat next to Julia, who was the only one – but all the more for that – who resembled Kira.

Firstly, several assets were redistributed within the family. Ted paid no attention to the details, except for when Julia was given the key to Kira's infamous study, where no one but her had ever been allowed in.

The publisher received an external hard drive with a small note attached that read *Max Frisch and The Code*.

The publisher looked at the note, clueless, and then tried several times in vain to open the hard drive on his laptop.

„If I were you, I wouldn't keep entering any more wrong passwords!"

Ted looked sternly at the publisher.

„Why not?"

„Well, the note ... I reckon the hard drive contains a book or several books, meant for publishing in twenty years."

„That's ... Why would you think that ...?"

„Well. There is a strikingly similar case in *The Code*. A hard drive secured in a way that if the wrong password is entered ten times, the content will be deleted; the password-protection though, expires after twenty years."

„I never read that book. That was before my time. You seem to know your way around her books."

„Yes. I have read all of them several times." Ted looked out of the window, smiling dreamily – He had read all of them in all likelihood twenty times.

„Yes, I think, I know them all by heart."

Ted could tell that the publisher took that for a joke, but continued anyway:

„She always admired Max Frisch and he too wrote a book, so close to him, that it was only to be published twenty years after his passing."

The publisher looked deeply frustrated at his hard drive and put the laptop away.

The notary turned to Ted:

„Miss Adams has left you a hard drive as well, Mr. Coffee."

The publisher laughed briefly: „But that makes little sense, because, all due respect ..., Mr. Coffee, you are seventy years old, if you will only be able to read this in twenty years ..."

„No, I think, I can crack the code."

Ted smiled to himself. He already had an idea what the password might be.

He was the first to leave the office and was mentally preparing the unlocking of the hard drive later at home:

Coffee – naturally – her cup and her jacket (time had not been kind on the fabric, but had done nothing to the memory), tiramisu, maybe a ...

„One moment please, Mr. Coffee!"

Julia came up behind him. Ted stopped. She looked at him sheepishly.

„Forgive me. I hope, you don't think of it as invasive. But, I would never forgive myself if I hadn't at least asked you ...

Would you maybe consider ... Could we talk, just for a little while? May I invite you for lunch or a drink, maybe?"

Ted liked Kira's daughter very much that is why he swallowed the words that had come to his mind spontaneously. He was really looking forward to being alone with the hard drive.

Julia bit her lip. She must have guessed the answer, without him saying anything.

"I'm sorry. I can imagine that you want to return home. But the flight back might be stressful, a little something might be good before ..."

Ted smiled ... and saw a glimmer of hope in Julia's eyes.

"I would so very much like to get to know you a little bit better! I know, you meant the world to my mother. She never said so but ... I think, you were James."

Ted smiled, not saying a word.

"You don't talk. You must be James!"

Ted laughed: "Okay. You win."

Julia beamed.

"Would you maybe like a very special coffee? A small, unknown coffee farm in Tanzania. My mother gave me the pack last year for my twentieth birthday. *For a special occasion*, she had added in writing. I don't want to drink it alone and I wouldn't know anyone else, who could understand my loss like you."

Ted nodded. "Yes ... gladly, absolutely, but only under the condition that you call me Ted, Julia."

"I'd love to, Ted!", said Julia beaming and hugged him.

They spent a very nice evening at the lake, bordering the property of the Adams family. For the most part, they drifted through the water on a boat, drank coffee and talked about Kira.

„She wrote a lot in her last weeks ..., probably to finish the James she had started, but she didn't manage it ..."

„Will it be published anyway?"

Julia blushed slightly:

„Mum had put in her will that I am to finish it and to continue the series. She was convinced that I could. She said, I am a lot like her."

„Yes, I share that opinion; not just from the looks of things."

Julia blushed even more.

„Thank you. Just before she passed, she told me that I could probably do it better than she herself, because I supposedly have the genes of a magnificent artist inside me."

„Your father is an artist too?"

„Dad? No, sadly not at all. A loving father, an extremely talented handyman and an excellent manager for mum, but nothing much to do with art at all. He never learned an instrument and only read a few of her books. It is simply not for him ... or both my older siblings. That's why mum was so happy, when I came into the family. I wasn't planned apparently; she was almost forty-eight, after all ..."

„Yes, at first I, too, thought you were one of the grandchildren, until you introduced yourself ..."

„Happens to me all the time. I actually have a nephew, who is older than me."

„I never introduced myself as James. How did you know?"

„Knowing is said too much. It was more of a hunch. Mum told me a lot about James these last few weeks, so I can continue the series; much about, how she envisions him, how he is sitting next to her, while drinking coffee ... It was all so detailed, so real ... More and more I came under the impression that he wasn't an entirely fictional character and when I saw you today ..., even though you only said a few words ... I had imagined him just like that ... Well, a bit younger maybe."

Both smiled.

The surface of the lake was perfectly placid, not even the tiniest of waves. Julia threw a small pebble into the water and for a long time they regarded the ripples it caused on the lake.

„I am happy that I got to meet you, James! You really are a normal and very likeable person. As a child, I was sometimes very jealous of James, when mum was singing his praises. In my imagination, he was an unsurmountable giant, who took my mum away from me."

„That was never my intention."

„Oh, nonsense. You never really took her away from me; on the contrary. You have enriched the lives of all of us. It just dawned on me over the last few weeks. Without you, mum would have never been this happy and she infected us all with her happiness. No ..., I had a very happy childhood and you were always there as well, somehow ... - classic James: Invisible, inaudible, but I felt you, when mum sat in the armchair and dreamily drank her coffee and recently, when I play the piano or write stories ..."

Ripples still creased the lake's surface; Ted smiled.

Julia had one hand drifting in the water.

„Was your mum happy?"

„Yes. Yes, very much. Of course, not all the time. But I never met anyone, who came even close to her taking life so laid back, who had such a contagious laugh, who quietly beamed to herself so much. She was happy, with us, her family, with writing, with life ..., but never were her eyes as bright as when she spoke of James ..."

The boat rocked lightly. A slightly bigger wave, gently creased, came towards them, as if the lake was smiling ...

Sip Nine

Ted unplugged the coffee machine and carried it from the kitchen into the living room, fixed up the first cup and then plugged the hard drive into his laptop.

2 of 10 attempts remain.

Apparently someone before him had tried to guess the password. Ted knew immediately what was meant with the hint: *A fish in salad, Eau de Cologne in ripples, a coffee in desert*.

He knew all her books, or at least line 11 on page 47 of each by heart. But since only two attempts remained, he wanted to make sure and had another look at her third novel *Ripples*, then he entered *Tuna, Without you I wouldn't have known what I was meant for, Tiramisu* and just like that the explorer opened and showed the contents of the hard drive ...

Ted had expected a text, a letter maybe, but before him were several folders, tons of word-documents, a few pictures, several videos.

Just to be sure, Ted got up and grabbed another pack of coffee-beans. It was going to be a long day for the coffee-machine.

First there was a brief introduction:

My beloved Ted,

it would have only taken me a few days more to finish James 27, but there are more important things; there is someone more important ...

I have published some of the countless stories and thoughts that I have written down over the last decades, but no one has ever seen my favourite books so far ...

I have collected them here for you and tried to get them a bit in order and maybe improve upon a few things ..., because ... with the stories about us, I am never fully content. In my life, I have found words for most things that I wanted to tell. The stories I crafted from experience were always larger, more beautiful and more exciting than the reality that inspired them; but everything I wrote about you, about us, seems to me so much weaker, compared to this unfathomable, eternally far and free surreality we shared together.

I would have loved to have written something that would unmistakeably express what you meant to me, what I was because of you.

The usual three words, I will not write, they have been said too many times and they express far too little and have been abused so many times for matters of no importance.

We did not share much in the real world, but so much more in infinite worlds and stories. We travelled dozens of countries, most likely have been to every beach and every café on earth. We played concerts together and, on the side, saved the world on numerous occasions ... - Reality? Oh, tish tosh!

A few wonderful real moments, full of magic and in between wonderful years, in which the tension never subsided, the desire never diminished. You better believe, we have done everything right!

You are the bliss that has never faded, that never became routine. With you I always had the magic, that lives in every new beginning.

The moment when first we met, when all questions are still unanswered, we managed to make it last a lifetime, the most beautiful and most inspiring of moments.

We did not have just one life together, we created hundreds for ourselves, in songs and books.

I had infinite riches in life, thanks to you. A few of those wonderful days with you, I have put into writing.

Yours, in all worlds loving and very happy,
Kira

The first folder contained eleven entries into a diary.

At the very beginning, the longest entry, from the evening after the night they had spent together at the Kyffhaus Hut.

She wrote about the coffee at seven p.m. and how good she had felt in her imagination next to him. A few thoughts about the night together. About waking up on his chest and his hand in hers and her confusion, whether Ted was her life and not Mirco, with whom she was happy and who had just told her that very day that he would get her out of there in a few short weeks, if everything went well with his scholarship for Sydney.

He had planned everything and so far she had looked forward to it, to finally escape this prison with him and now ... She could finally run, on foot with her boyfriend, but suddenly the opportunity had opened up to fly, discover all new worlds, with a big, unknown bird, who had grabbed her softly with his talons last night and had carried her through heights unknown ...

Was a life on Ted's side, as his piano teacher and partner, possible?

And then, out of nowhere, a long story ran its course, an almost completed book. It had strong similarities with her first big success 'If you had stayed', only a much more subjective and more personal version.

It had been her muse's kiss. Previously she had never felt like writing more than her diary and in that too never more than what had really happened ...

Another entry was from the year prior to the Oscars, written in between, on one of their few days together, at the editing of the music for the film:

When I'm sitting here next to you, we never touch, we have hardly ever touched earnestly, and also the things said never touch the true feelings that I harbour for you ...

We are good friends, both loyal, at least physically, to our respective partners and yet always that undeniable feeling:

We know each other on a different level. We have been together all this time. That feeling of coming home, when I open the door and you are sitting there, smiling.

The touch of your body, soft caresses and passionate kisses ..., always present as a wish, but strangely as a memory too, as something known ...

There is not only the life in the real world. There are dreams, fantasies, infinite possibilities outside of reality, which sets us such tight limitations, that annoys with gravity and fatigue. In here is only a single book; out there is the great library.

Can it be that we are together in a parallel world and our bliss is shining from there onto us here, that we are somehow, almost intangibly connected to our parallel selves? So many religions believe in a life after death that is somehow timeless. Why not have several lifes at once in different worlds ... simultaneously? Time, after all, does not really exist.

Our shared world really does exist, whenever and wherever it may be.

I will never be able, in this life, to fully explain it or at least decently describe it, but I clearly feel it:

I am in that other world, in which I am together with you, a very happy woman!

Ted had relocated his reading from the dining table to the bed, because his eyes were falling shut again and again, after, by now, seven hours of reading, and he slept briefly in between, had wonderful dreams and then read on.

Often he would lie down after especially beautiful passages, close his eyes and would feel Kira's head on his chest ...

It goes without saying that by now the coffee-machine was standing near the bed and an empty pack of coffee-beans was next to his pillow.

Other items had been added, a big pack of tissues, because Ted, who had never cried much in his life, had to blow his nose now quite a lot because of how touched he was and had to wipe away many tears of joy.

After an entry about Christmas, ten years ago, Ted needed a whole pack:

Sometimes I feel, like I am living in my stories already and that here on earth, in this barren study, is simply my workplace as an author. I make it through my workload and then it is quitting time, away from the tight study, out in the infinitely wide world of dreams and stories, where the most beautiful part of my life is happening ...

Just after one in the morning, somewhere between Christmas and Boxing-day, a starry night and a full moon ...

Up until a moment ago I was sitting, after a rich Christmas dinner and a lot of delicious red wine, in the warm, comfy sitting-room and all of a sudden, I felt the urge to go outside right now and to walk with you, hand in hand, through this wonderful night ..., in the honest belief that I only needed this one mile, this half hour with you maybe and everything would be fine for a long, long time, maybe forever, at the very least for a few weeks ...

Everything would be healed, filled with happiness or at least easily bearable, because all the, oftentimes, hard-to-bear reality would be outshined, because I would constantly feel your hand in mine, every now and then taking a glance at you, at your beautiful silhouette in the moonlight ...

You were so close to me, like no one has ever been in the real world, when I walked with you, just a moment ago, knowing that you're not really there but also knowing that I feel you right there next to me ... and that reality really isn't what counts in my life ...

I am quite drunk and happy about it, because it gives me an excuse, not being able to describe, how amazing this stroll with you has been, how much strength it gave me in the real world, of which you are sadly too rarely a part and yet you permeate it and leave more of an impression and happiness and strength to go on, than all the other important, present people around me ...

You are the best thing that has ever happened to me!

He had finished the diaries. The second folder was even more expansive:

Eleven unpublished, finished books and several incomplete fragments.

A series about the both of them; their life together, how it could have been, if they had ended up together, all those years ago.

With joyful levity she talked of decades of big, unburdened love, full of freedom, travels, cuddling and with ample amounts of music and books.

Shared artistic creations. Her writing, while he is playing the piano, somewhere in a small cabin, far from civilization. They may not be rich but have enough to live happily together: Music, literature, cosy furniture and really good coffee ...

In another book, their situation, how it really had played out: They had met only a few times but had enriched and shaped each other's life.

After her husband had passed, Ted and Kira, both now well over seventy, finally come together.

Shortly after though, Kira is diagnosed with onset dementia. To slow down its progress, they tell each other their memories. In the beginning, both from their separate lives but later on it more and more blurs into one.

They sit in front of the fireplace, drink coffee and tell and remember the few real things and the loads of dreams.

At some point she only addresses Ted as her husband and keeps telling him how happy her life with him was ...

Ted glances over it most times but on one occasion he actually says:

„Oh, Kira, how I would have loved to be your husband! How I would have loved to have experienced all these things with you; how happy I would have been, to have woken up next to you every morning, but for most of our lives sadly, we haven't been together ...“

„Oh, my dear Ted, you are a bit confused again. I can't re-member a single day in my life, where we weren't together!"

Kira beams at him. Ted nods and smiles.

„Yes. You are right actually. I feel the same way. I couldn't have said it better myself."

After a folder with many unpublished letters to James and one with pictures, came a folder with several films:

When he came to *The Bridges of Madison County* he gave up on the tissues and just got out of his wet clothes afterwards.

Many of the films, Ted had already watched, some (e.g. *The Light*) were new to him.

The last one was a clip from *Bambi*:

The autumn wind was blowing the leaves from a tree.

At the end only two were left, which seem to dance with each other, then one breaks loose and falls, after waving back and forth, to the ground. The other now sees no more sense in staying on the tree and makes its way down in a similar fashion and lands next to the other leaf.

Ted had spent almost three weeks in his home, mainly in the bedroom; now he went out in the garden, took in the fresh air and sat down in the garden-swing.

He had a sip of coffee, set down the cup next to him and instead took the printed-out version of his favourite letter to James in his hands.

My beloved spring-sun!

Oh, what happy weeks filled with sunshine, warmth and soothing wind we had, what a wonderful May!

Soon summer will be here and all of a sudden you disappear behind a cloud and I hear you say:

I mean nothing, one of many, nothing special ... - and I, cheery tree in full bloom, shake my branches in disbelief and beam at my spring-sun with glowing buds:

You are not the sun that shines the hottest;

and not the one, gracing the sky the longest;

not the one, producing the tackiest dawns and dusks ...

You are one sun of many in the year ..., but you are my favourite sun!

You give the first warmth after a long grey autumn and icy winter, wake up frozen over dreams and hopes back to life and touch with your unique rays my soul's buds and I blossom with an indescribable feeling of joy ...

Here and now and for these days, you mean, my dearest spring-sun, everything for me!

...and in weeks and months that follow, when I need the rain and other suns again ...:

I will always, my entire tree-life long, think of you, my first sun that woke me up, that made me blossom;

and every year anew, I will, in stormy autumn and saddest winter, hope for you and await longingly your rays ...

Epilogue

Ted read Kira's letter that Julia had sent him just a few days ago, once more. She had found him in the secret room, with the instructions to send it to Ted this week:

My beloved Ted,

hundreds of people, with whom I had many dealings over the years, a few dozens, with whom I lived together for a while on a daily basis ... Those, who are still alive and up for it, will come to the farewell-party.

Most of them think they know me, some of them think they know everything about me. My life had been under constant scrutiny over the past few decades; a lot has been written about it ... - About the things that really defined me, hardly anybody knew.

We both sadly only met a few times in real life and yet ...:

We had, right in the middle of the bustling of almost ten billion people on this planet, a small world all our own, that no one knew about.

Even today, when my body is not working anymore and I mainly feel tired, I have an invigorating exhilaration in me, when I think of our secret places. Suddenly I feel the urge to write one more book, but no, I really have finished, want to go this way to the end and wait there for you ...

No more books ..., only a small greeting and a few directions. To you, who meant the world to me ...

The directions are simple: Go to that little farewell-party, I organised in Bremen. You will know the place ...

> *Love,*
>
> *Your Kira*

In her affairs Kira had organised a mourning service, no, she had insisted, not a mourning service, but instead a happy farewell-party for her friends and family in Germany. She was set for seven weeks after her funeral; on the first of July, when Kira would have turned sixty-nine years old.

Why Kira had chosen the restaurant – *Ständige Vertretung* - in Bremen, for her farewell-party, no one could really make sense of. She had never read any of her works there or had even ever been there to begin with, as far as everyone knew.

Even Ted, who knew that he was privy to a lot of things no one else knew about her, did not understand at first, why she had chosen that location, until he passed by a café on his way there and saw, which kind of coffee was served there.

Okay, I recognised our place ... But ..., why not here then?

When he arrived at the *Ständige Vertretung*, which was brimming with people in spite of its size, he realized why the party was not held at the small café.

He sat down at a table and took a look around: It had to be hundreds of people. Not exactly what he liked ... Why had Kira asked him to come here? Was he supposed to directly go to the café?

An elderly waitress walked up to his table.

„Mr. Coffee! I am so happy to see you again!"

Indeed, she did look familiar.

„Do you remember me? Katja. The hotel in Sydney? The roof-terrace?"

„Yes ..., of course! Katja. Forgive me. I'm a bit older now and not as quick as I used to be ... I'm happy too!"

He stood up and they hugged.

103

„I never really knew what had become of you both, up there on the roof, followed books and songs, never fully sure, always hoped though ... and then I receive this letter from Australia – Kimberly Rachel Adams asks in her will for me to work here tonight ... She actually had written a small letter to me. I am supposed to keep a special eye on one of the customers ...“

She winked happily. Ted again felt his eyes welling up with tears of emotion. It really had ramped up recently! Katja handed him a tissue.

„Now, James, first of all, have a seat and a coffee on the lady!“

„Thank you!“

It was not *Machare,* but the coffee here tasted very good as well. Ted closed his eyes and drank; the noisy party disappeared immediately and, in his mind, he was in happy memories with the celebrity.

Katja brought him with his second coffee a home-made tiramisu and later on a tuna-salad. Kira had enclosed the recipes in her letter.

The party too turned out quite nicely later on. Julia talked to him briefly and was excited to tell him, how easy it was for her to continue writing the James-novels, now that she had met him.

Later on Katja sat down at his table for quite some time. She had a very nice, smooth voice, he had not noticed years ago.

What exactly she told him, Ted did not catch in its entirety. Gradually over the last few months and rapidly these last few days, he less and less noticed what was going on around him. That only happened to him earlier in his life when he was making music. Now it happened constantly in the everyday world. Had he developed dementia? Unlikely. The short-term memory would have worked perfectly fine, if he had wanted it to, if he had any stock left in the present ... He simply loved to live in his past and his dreams, where his collected bodily aches did not yet exist and where Kira was still part of this world ...

After a few short speeches was a break and Ted first went into the restroom and then outside to catch some fresh air.

Julia came out as well.

„Ah, there you are, Ted. I completely forgot about it a moment ago. There is still something for you."

She handed him a small package.

„Here, I found this in the small room, which mum gave to me in her will. She had a note attached to it, telling me, to give it to you today."

All of a sudden Ted was once more fully in the here and now. He sat down in a chair and with calm hands, but with a soul shaking in excitement, he opened the package.

It was her coffee-cup with Linus and his blankey on it, which had always been with her at every reading or any other public appearance.

Under the cup was a folded letter. Ted noticed, while unfolding it that she had sprayed it with her coffee aroma.

He smelled it for a moment with his eyes closed and then read:

I never took care of anything as much, as I have of this cup; even though I have taken good care of my children as well, like a good mother ...

A week ago, I drank a pot of coffee from this cup and with every sip have tasted our lives once more. I do not know, whether in the moment of my death, my life will play out like a film before me, if so, I would like it to be this exact one ...

I can't think of a more fulfilled life, than the one we shared!

Of course you know, who I meant with the two leaves on the autumn tree in Bambi. A treelife long we were next to each other but really touched each other only briefly when the wind allowed us to. Now I'm falling to the ground. I will look for a place, where there are no other leaves, a place all our own ...

...and you will find me, and we will be together ...

I don't know when and how and haven't got any idea in what shape ..., but no matter where: I will see you again! And exactly there will be my heaven!

I am looking forward to us ...

Ted folded her letter up and put it in his breast-pocket, so close to his wildly beating heart ...

He wiped away a tear from his left eye and stood up.

Julia smiled:

„Seems to be something truly beautiful ... You coming back inside again? It would be great if you could play something on the piano."

Ted looked at her cordial but shook his head.

„No ... No, really, I can't. The arthritis. I can't do it as well anymore, as this moment deserves ... No. I would like to be alone for a moment."

„But it is cold out here and there is really good coffee inside! I'm sure I can tempt you with that?"

„Yes. Normally you would ..., but not right now. But thanks anyway. Thanks for everything! I'll take a quick stroll ... and afterwards ... We'll see each other again ..."

Julia nodded and went back inside. She assumed that Ted had meant him and herself when he had said *each other* ...

Ted nodded after her amicably and then went to the café in the market square.

He sat down in the sun, set down Kira's cup in front of him and ordered a large pot of coffee and a small jug of milk ...